For my dearest Gabriela, without whom I would be lost and bereft. Your love, grace, wit, courage, and tenderness have, and continue to be, the magic that warms my soul and gives me the courage always to be better. You are the Angel of my Life.

– With Love J.P.

J.P. Johnson

THE PANACEA OF LIFE

The Vines that Bind

AUSTIN MACAULEY PUBLISHERS®
LONDON * CAMBRIDGE * NEW YORK * SHARJAH

This is a work of fiction. Names, characters, businesses, places, events, locales, and incidents are either the products of the author's imagination or used in a fictitious manner. Any resemblance to actual persons, living or dead, or actual events is purely coincidental.

Ordering Information
Quantity sales: special discounts are available on quantity purchases by corporations, associations, and others. For details, contact the publisher at the address below.

Publisher's Cataloging-in-Publication data
Johnson, J.P.
The Panacea of Life

ISBN 9781647500481 (Paperback)
ISBN 9781647500474 (Hardback)
ISBN 9781647500498 (ePub e-book)

Library of Congress Control Number: 2023922897

www.austinmacauley.com/us

First Published 2024
Austin Macauley Publishers LLC
40 Wall Street, 33rd Floor, Suite 3302
New York, NY 10005
USA

mail-usa@austinmacauley.com
+1 (646) 5125767

Foreword

My Heart Has No Soul

My Purpose before me
My conquest in sight
A captain of destiny
Never scared of the fight

I charge to the ramparts
Victorious the fight
I will conquer my demons
Through wisdom and might

My soul is a stone
My soul is a stone

Like a needle to a compass
I knew my own course
I gladly paid the price
Never counting the cost

Confident and resolute
I stood face in the wind
Like the stone of the pillar
I shall never give in

No fear or no challenge
Would waver my sight
No regrets and no sorrows
Would assuage this great fight
My soul is a stone
My soul is a stone

Like water is to granite
A silent cry turns to tears
My purpose has failed me
These chains of long years

Bursting from the pressure
From the years of the pain
The stone cracks into pieces
Till nothing remains

My soul was a stone
My soul becomes dust

Like an Angel of Mercy
She swept in like a flame
The compassion she gave me
For the dust that remained

Gentle hands and forgiveness
The tools of her trade
With time and persistence
The dust was remade

My soul, which was stone
And then became dust
My soul that's been remade
My soul that's been saved

My soul is my heart
My heart is my soul

Chapter 1

Waking up, I found myself wondering what the day would bring. It was sunny but cool, and there was a hint of autumn in the air. The leaves rustled in the breeze and cast shadows on my bedroom wall like they were telling a story. It was an odd feeling. I had never woken up without anything I had to do, nowhere to be, or a phone call to get on. The absence of this was unsettling.

I had spent all my adult life becoming someone I didn't know. Sure, I had been a successful entrepreneur and built many companies, but now that I had sold my last one just the prior day, I felt an urge not to repeat what I had become so accustomed to doing—find a company, buy it, fix it, and sell it. The cycle was monotonous, and I was lost in this rinse-and-repeat world I had created for myself.

A thought, almost a fear, crossed my mind: what should I do? What could I do? I had never asked myself this question. I hurriedly jumped out of bed and pushed those bewildering thoughts out of my head. I quickly hopped into the shower and then jumped in my car to rush to a local coffee shop to give myself something to do.

Arriving at the coffee shop, the baristas who knew me well as I was there virtually every day greeted me with my usual tea and pastry; they were such kind people. I left a 100-dollar tip in the jar for all the times they had tolerated me. Valerie grabbed my hand as I turned to go to my regular spot in the corner and whispered in my ear, "You know, that is 100 dollars!"

I smiled and told her, "Yes, indeed." I did know, and I hoped she and Ellie would split it. She came from behind the counter and hugged me, which was unexpected but pleasant.

Once I sat down, I struggled to figure out what to do with myself after a few minutes of trying to read a local newspaper and then surfing the news on my phone. Later, Ellie came over and sat down. She asked me what was troubling me, and I was a bit taken aback. Ellie was a reticent girl who rarely spoke to me. But something I had said or even done made her concerned for my well-being. I told her I was okay, that I had just sold my company the day before and was retired, but I was only 50 and had no idea what was next. Oh my God, I said it, the word I had feared for as long as I could remember. She smiled.

"Congrats!"

She then hugged me and asked what I was going to do now. I honestly did not know. I shrugged my shoulders and gave her a puzzled look. She smiled again.

"You will figure it out; you are a smart guy and pretty handsome for an older gentleman."

I must have blushed; she giggled as she walked away. Such a beautiful woman like that had not spoken to me in a long time. As a divorced man, I had put love and romance in the rearview mirror. But, at that moment, I realized I was unhappy. Now that I am financially secure, it might be time for me to try and find a happier life for myself. I quickly got up, walked over to Ellie, thanked her, and kissed her cheek. She was stunned, but as I turned to walk out, she shouted, "Have a wonderful day!"

After leaving the coffee shop, I raced home to hatch my plan, though I had no idea what that plan would be. As I sat at my desk, staring out over the view of the lake below, I had no idea what I would do. I was restless; I could not sit for more than five minutes without creating some menial tasks to occupy my mind. This went on for days. I needed help figuring out where to start. I was stuck, like a car in the mud. I could not go forward, and there was no turning back. I almost resigned from saying that this was as good as it would get. I tried picking up some of my old hobbies: golf, fishing, and working on my estate. But I was still restless!

Ellie asked how it was going one morning at the coffee shop, and I spilled the beans. I was miserable, and I had no idea what to do with myself.

"Hell, I am not ready to retire! I have another twenty or so good years left in me," I stated emphatically.

"*Do you need to work?*"

I smiled and responded that money was not the issue. I had more than I deserved. She looked at me with a puzzled look, then yelled at me, "Then what the hell is your problem, man? You have money, a beautiful home, and cars; you can travel and see the world. You know how fucking lucky you are?"

I sat awash with anger at how she spoke to me, but then I realized she was right. She must have seen something in my eyes, maybe a tear; I honestly don't know. She came around the table, hugged me from behind, and then asked me the most challenging question, "Do you have someone in your life, someone you love?"

I trembled as I told her that, in fact, no, I had given up on love many years ago. She asked me why. I knew this would be a long and complicated story, but I did my best to surmise the situation as it was.

She was stunned to find out I had been married, that she even worked with me, and that I had treated them so kindly. I told her it was not their fault we got divorced; it was mine. I had never been honest with any of them.

"Not honest… How so?"

After a long pause, I explained that as a young man, I had met someone, and I had never found another like her: passionate, loving, kind, gentle—

She interrupted me, "Where is she?"

"What?" I responded, not hearing what she had just asked.

She repeated herself, "Where is this dream girl?"

I told her it was complicated. She had married, and even though we would meet from time to time for short vacations together, we both had other lives.

"Fuck that!" she said. "If she was all you say she was, you need to go. You need to go now and find her." I didn't have the heart to tell her that years prior, Francesca had been tragically killed in an accident. But maybe she was right. Perhaps I needed to return to where my heart and passion had been set ablaze so many years ago.

Chapter 2

It had been years since I had been to Italy. I had taken some vacations there but had not been there alone or with Francesca in many years. But somewhere deep inside, I knew this was what I needed to do. I spent the rest of the day preparing my plans and packing my bags. I got my travel arrangements taken care of and even arranged to purchase a car once I arrived.

I had always wanted a Ferrari Dino, and they were so hard to find, but I located one in a little town near Modena, just west of Bologna. I decided to fly to London and take the Eurostar to Paris. From there, I would grab the TGV to Genoa and pick up a rental car to drive to Modena. I had an old friend in the area; she said I was welcome to crash at her place while I purchased the vehicle and got all the necessary permits. So, there it was, and I had the beginnings of a plan. On the path at last, I thought to myself as I locked the doors, got in my car, and drove to the airport.

Once I arrived at my friend's house, I quickly got busy with the car and the paperwork. She asked me what my plan was. When I told her why I had come, she laughed.

"*Yeah, you have been bitten by the bug.*"

"The bug?" I asked. "What bug?"

"*We Italian women are special; once you have been bitten by one of us, you will always desire to be with us,*" she replied.

I thought how true that was; though I had many lovers, nothing compared to the Italian beauties I had met. I sheepishly grinned and acknowledged that there was some truth in what she had said. She asked if I had a plan now that I was in the country. I told her I thought I would drive back to the little village where I had first met Francesca, or as she would put it, *where I had been bitten*. She agreed. It was a good start, but she warned me I would need help finding what I was looking for there.

"You have to open yourself up to fate, expose your soul to all you see and feel. Then, and only then, will fate set you on your course," she said.

Sophie was a wonderful lady, but her husband had traveled for his work for me for years. On more than one occasion, she had made it known that even though she loved him, she was always searching for a next lover like many Italian women. But even with all that encouragement, it still was not what I desired. She was gorgeous and had a dry sense of humor. She told me many stories about her conquests as a young girl, even some of her recent ones. She was always vivid with her stories and never left me without a great mental picture and maybe a few of my own desires, I have to admit.

The next day, I finally got the car; it was beautiful, just as I had always imagined. As I got in the car, Sophia smiled and said, "I hope you know that car will not make love to you."

I laughed. "I know, but if I am going to drive, I might as well drive in style."

She leaned into the car and gave me a big kiss, wishing me the best of fortune and telling me I was always welcome at her place. As I pulled away, she yelled, "Don't forget to try the wine!"

Even with all that, I felt apprehensive about the adventure I was embarking upon. Would I find something to give me purpose, would fate steer me on a course to happiness, and would I find that ever-elusive panacea to calm my restless spirit? Only time will tell.

Interlude
My Beloved Francesca

When I was a young man, I was a wonderfully talented musician. I loved to perform and would try to sing and play somewhere almost every week. I was invited to go to Europe and spend eight weeks traveling and performing. Now that I look back on it, it was my first tour.

At the time, I was performing operatic style with an orchestra in halls, and at night, I would perform in a small band in small clubs. It was all new to me, coming from the Bible Belt of America. I had never even been inside a bar other than a country club. It was such a heady atmosphere; the personalities were so vibrant, and the way people dressed, their tattoos, and the way they spoke was like visiting a foreign planet more than a foreign country. It was there that I had my first taste of alcohol.

In America, other than stealing from my parent's liquor cabinet, you could not get a drink until you were 21. Vienna had no drinking age, and we spent our first week there. I still remember that hard cider, even though it is a blur. It was excellent, and the feeling was just so relaxing. I had my first cigarette and my first joint as well that fateful fun week. I would get all cleaned up every morning and head off to perform at some hall; one day, I even got invited to perform at the Rat House for the President of Austria and his wife.

But by night, that was when my true nature would appear, like a butterfly from a cocoon. As soon as the streets turned dark, things got crazy. This was the age of everything, from disco to rock. You could be anything. We would dress up, put on makeup, and hit the clubs. We played a few sets every night somewhere and then danced and partied until near dawn. It was a new world for me and one I had never expected to find.

Every few days, we would move to another city and play in the halls during the day and at the clubs at night. Each of these stops had its mystery. The people were different yet the same. We continued for about four weeks when we found ourselves without any gigs for over a week. Nothing was wrong; it was just a break between Lienz and Salzburg. The director who was overseeing our travel itinerary picked us up some bar gigs in a little town in Northern Italy.

He told us to tone it down, as it would be a bit more conservative, so we would need to put away the stage personas we had developed over the past month. Honestly, that was okay, but I was getting tired, as it felt like every night, it turned into a Vaudeville-type production.

So, the other two guys I played with bailed on the gigs, and I ended up doing piano and acoustic sets for the next week. It was a significant change from the prog-rock we had been belting out the prior weeks. We ended up in this little town called Brunico, where we were staying and playing at the bar at a resort. I think it was a stay-and-play deal. Now that I look back on it, I think we were all pretty broke by then.

It was here that I first saw her. She was the owner, well, her family was the owner, but during the summer, she would come up to the mountains while her husband stayed back in the city. I can still remember the first time I saw her; it was so vivid in my mind. It is like a dream…

After performing my first set, I sat in a booth towards the back of the place near the kitchen. She was sitting at the table just in front of me, close enough to observe but not so close I would have been able to talk to her. I remember thinking about how wondrous she looked. I had never seen someone that looked like her. Her hair was long and draped down her back like a cape. She had these magical eyes that captivated me, and then there were the lips. They were full and red, but not fake like from lipstick. They were deep, burgundy, luxurious lips.

She had a smile that was both whimsical and mischievous when she flashed it at someone. I was hypnotized. I remember thinking I needed to write a song about her, about those lips. As I sat there watching her drink her glass of wine, the redness of the wine graced her lips, much like a lover's kiss. It made me jealous, though I could not understand why.

Why does the wine get to kiss her divine lips and not me? I was thinking as I sat and watched her swirl the glass while the wine followed her every motion. Like she is teasing it, the wine waits with anticipation beyond measure for the next time it will once again touch her lips. She sips the wine again, but it is never enough to satisfy the lust for her the wine is feeling. By then, she had noticed I was watching, to which I was oblivious; a bomb could have gone off, and I would not have heard it.

But she knew I was. She started exaggerating her performance, letting the wine linger on her lips and then using the tip of her tongue to lick what little bit of wine was left on her upper lip. I was lost in her lips and the wine she was teasing them with. Just then, she lifted that glass gave it a swirl, and swallowed what was left. I am not sure what I did, but the next thing I remember was her tapping my table.

"Hey…you there?" Laughing at me. "It is time for your next set."

What? I thought, *Oh yeah, I need to perform again.* I got up and walked to the stage. I spent that entire set singing to her; I don't think I looked at a single other person in the place; I am not even sure there was anyone else there but me, her, and her lips.

When I finished that night, I went back to the small room they had put us up in. It was a small cabin with one bed and a couch. The problem was that there were three of us. I told the guys about the woman with the lips. They teased me to the point that I got mad and stormed out of the room. After walking around the property, I went back to the room, but they had locked me out.

I was sick of their teasing, and I could find somewhere else; it would not be my first, nor my last time, not having a bed to sleep in. In the past, when I had nowhere to sleep, I would look at places like barns, clubhouses, pools, or beaches. The closest thing I could find here was a spa area; thankfully, it was still open. It was lovely, and I was sweaty from performing earlier, so I was happy to shower and get cleaned up.

I had changed clothes back in the room but had not had a chance to shower. When I got out of the shower, I decided to sit in the sauna and try to relax. I wanted to continue my dream of those lips, so I threw my clothes in a locker, grabbed a towel, and went in.

I had been in the sauna for several minutes when the door opened. I was slightly startled, as I thought I was the only one still up and moving, as it was sometime after 2 a.m. I leaned back, closed my eyes, and did not pay attention to who had come in.

I was in a zone, dreaming of those lips, and lost in my thoughts when she first spoke. I almost thought it was an angel in my dreams speaking to me. I was lost in my world. I had been humming and singing some unknown tune that my heart was creating. Somewhere in all of it, I must have started putting some prose into my thoughts.

"Hey…Hey, snap out of it."

That is when she popped me on the head, causing me to jump out of my skin; it jolted me and scared the shit out of me. I jumped up so fast that I did not realize my towel had fallen off me. It was her; I was staring at those lips again; I could not stop.

"*You might want to cover yourself.*" It was then I realized I was naked standing in front of her and was very aroused from the dream state I had been in; after all, I was a young man, so I guess it was normal.

Well… My God, I am still standing there; I cannot move.

"*Here take this*", As she handed me my towel, I took it and stood there. I was frozen, not out of fear, but frozen just the same.

"*Do I need to cover you myself?*"

Finally, I got control of myself and wrapped the towel around my waist.

She started laughing. "*You know, you probably should have been in the men's locker room.*"

"WHAT?"

"*You are in the ladies' locker room.*"

"Please, tell me you are kidding me?"

"*Nope, wish I was.*"

"I am so sorry, I will leave."

"*No, you do not have to do that. Plus, it is locked already, and I do not want to get out and let you in. Just have a seat and keep that thing under control.*" She laughed and pointed for me to sit next to her. I sat next to her, but I think I must have been shaking as she put her hand on my leg and told me to relax and that she would not devour me like she had the wine earlier that night.

"Fuck, you saw me?"

"*Well, yes, as did half the bar; you made quite the scene.*"

"Oh, dear, now I am embarrassed."

"*No, it is fine, but you must tell me what you were thinking. It was delicious based on the sounds you were making.*"

"SOUNDS I WAS MAKING! Oh God, I didn't; please tell me you're kidding."

"*Wish I could, but you were...well, let's just say having a moment with someone or something, and it appeared that I might have been somehow involved.*"

I thought honesty would be the best way out of this mess, plus I could claim I was being an artist. "Well, honestly, I guess you could say I was hypnotized, yes, hypnotized by your lips. Yes, with your lips and the interplay you had with your wine."

"*You mean to tell me that how I drank my wine caused all that?*"

"Honestly, yes, it did, I guess."

"*Well then, you must tell me what was so hypnotizing about my lips and the wine?*"

I sat there and told her about how I was jealous of the wine, the way it kissed her lips, and the way she teased it. I told her all, though I do not know why. I just went on and on and ON...

"*You have never kissed a woman, have you?*"

"Sure, I have; I have kissed several girls."

"*I did not ask if you had kissed a girl; I asked if you had kissed a woman.*"

"Oh...is there a difference?"

She burst out laughing. "*Oh, my boy, you have so much to learn, so much to learn. Yes, there is a big difference between kissing a girl and kissing a woman.*"

"Really, what makes it different? I do not see why it would be so different."

Then, out of nowhere: "*Well, I guess I will have to show you.*"

And with that, she kissed me for the first time. It was one of those surreal moments you can never forget, like a tattoo that can't be removed. I remember thinking, Oh God, her lips taste as divine as I had dreamed. Then, as quickly as it happened, it was over.

"*Now you see the difference.*"

I must have looked completely blank. I was still processing everything that had just happened. It was overwhelming; I was touched to the core of my being. She laughed.

"*Oh my, I can't believe I did that; what came over me?*"

"Maybe when you saw me naked, you could not resist!"

She started laughing so hard that she could not stop. As if what I had said before was not foolish enough, I had to open my big mouth again. Oh, why must I do this? I was thinking, but I could not stop.

"Well, you certainly did not seem to be in any rush for me to cover myself; admit it, I looked like Michelangelo's David." Oh God, I did not just say that.

She only started crowing louder and louder. I got up, ripped my towel off, and did my best pose. It only made things worse, and by this time, she was crying from laughing at me so much. Finally, I sat down, not knowing what to do. I just sat stewing in my misery. I had no words to express the situation. I had to endure the ridicule.

"*You might want to cover that thing up.*"

Fuck, I was in such a flummox I had forgotten to put my towel back around my waist. I must have been as red as a radish from the embarrassment. A few moments later, "*What will I do with you? You have so much spirit. It is a shame to let it all go to waste.*" I looked at her, puzzled; then it happened—she leaned in. "*We Italian women are always looking for our next lover. Kiss me.*" I lunged at the chance. I would not miss out on kissing her, kissing those lips again.

Over the following days, Francesca taught me all the pleasures of being a man and how to treat a woman with the most excellent care. I fell madly in love. I asked her why she had chosen me. She just smiled. *"I love my husband; he is a good man, but sometimes good men cannot handle all the passions us Italian women require. Remember, Nathan, I do love you, but not in the way I love my husband. You are fun and playful, and I can be someone with you that I cannot be with him. I hope we stay in touch, and maybe we will meet again; you can never tell where that starry map will lead."*

And with that, she kissed me and left. I was devastated. I knew I had been the lucky recipient of a unique, secret touch of the heart. We stayed in contact for many years, and our maps occasionally crossed. But then, our starry map was shattered.

Chapter 3

I had always thought of this place in a very spiritual context, even though I was not religious. It had been where I had crossed the threshold of being a man. I accidentally found my first love here when I was staying here many years ago. I had traveled here when I was a young musician. This is where I met her, Francesca. I hardly speak her name, as it feels like I am speaking of a Goddess. Ever since her tragic death many years ago, I could not bring myself to say her name. But now, in this place, I could speak it and even remember things I had pushed out of my mind so long ago.

The little pub and resort place she had once worked at had been bought by someone else, and they had completely renovated it. I stopped in to see what the new place looked like; I could stay the night. I decided to have a beer and get a bite to eat, but the place was as foreign as any restaurant in any town anywhere.

After eating, I walked around the property to see if I could catch a glimpse of where she had *bitten me*, as Sophia would put it. But it was nowhere to be found. I was depressed and saddened all over again. It was like losing her all over again. Why did I come here? I thought, why am I putting myself through this agony and pain? I decided I would not stay, but it was getting late, so I would have to drive to the next village and find a place to rest for the night.

As I left the parking lot, the rain started to fall; it was like the Gods knew the storm that was raging in my soul; it only seemed to add to the pain my heart felt. Pulling into the next village, I was able to locate a place to stay for the night. I took my stuff up to my room and laid on the bed, and for the first time that I could remember, I completely broke down into tears. My soul had broken into so many pieces I could no longer suppress the pain. It had been twenty or more years since I had been overwhelmed with so much anguish.

After a bit, I regained my composure, cleaned up, and decided to wander around and see if I could find a beer to drown my sorrows or even a good glass of wine. After all, Sophia had told me to *try the wine*! I decided that is what I would do. I would try the wine.

Finding a nice, quaint place to eat, I ordered the local special. I am not even sure what I ordered, but at that point, I honestly didn't care. I also made sure to order the wine... She brought over a local vintage with my dinner. I sat there sipping my wine and eating my dinner. I'm not sure how good it was, but I certainly kept asking for more wine.

I should have known better, but I didn't care at that moment. Over the evening, a few glasses of wine became a few bottles. After a while, my waitress informed me they were closing, and I would have to leave. I looked around to see I was the only person in the place. I was horrified at my behavior. I quickly paid my bill, leaving a huge tip. After leaving the restaurant, I staggered back to my room, collapsed onto the bed, and drifted off into a wine-influenced tormented sleep.

The following day, I awoke to a raging headache and overall feeling pretty much like I had been hit by a car. I gathered my things and made my way to the car, unsure where to head next. I knew I had to keep moving as staying here was going to be more painful than I could handle then.

Crawling into the car, I turned left out of the parking lot, heading opposite from the village where I had met Francesca. Over the next several weeks, I drove day and night, stopping to sleep, eat, and drink, but I could not find peace. Most days, I didn't even know which way I had driven or where I had stayed the night before.

I was a traveling spirit with no soul and no purpose; I was a wandering madman in the desert of life. Every day, I would drive in any direction, find somewhere to stay, drink all the wine I could get served, pass out in my room, get up the next day, and repeat the process.

One day, I stopped at a scenic lookout somewhere in the Italian Alps. I decided to walk down the trail to where the view would be better. I had picked up a camera and a journal in a village a few days prior. I had decided I would at least attempt to record where I was and where I had been, if for no other purpose than letting the authorities know who to notify if I became a victim of some tragic fate, maybe even at my own hands.

When I finally reached the trail's end, I was tired and completely out of breath; I saw a spring at the base of a rock. It was ironic somehow, in the turmoil of that day, I found some clarity. As I bent over to get a drink of water, I thought I cannot filter this water; it could be contaminated. Then I realized I no longer cared. If that water would be my demise, at least my thirst would be quenched. I crawled up the massive rock, which was not typically possible for me as I had a fear of heights since I was a child. But today, I never felt it; it was like I did not care if I fell from the wall. I did not want to get hurt or, worse, die, but I had stopped caring.

When I reached the top, I gazed out over the vast horizon. I had filled the bottle I was carrying with water from spring, and I decided I would drink and let fate take its course. I knew at this moment it was time for me to get busy living or get busy dying. I could no longer wander the wilderness in search of something that I could not even comprehend or imagine. As I thought to myself on that ledge, it would be so easy just to let myself slip off the edge; they would never find me, and I could fade from memory, nevermore to be haunted by the things that could have been, or care about the things that should have been. I could merely vanish like so many before me.

I sat there for hours, not sure what I was going to do. The only solace I could find was the knowledge that no matter what I decided, I knew I would not keep doing what I was doing and expect something to change. Like the millions of decisions I had made throughout my life, I had made them thinking they would lead me to happiness. Now, they were all just ghosts that haunted and tormented my dreams, giving me no peace.

Maybe there is no such thing as destiny, maybe there is no such thing as fate, but if not those, what could there be? Could love be what I was missing? I knew then that I needed to surrender myself to carry on and fight. I stood up and shouted as loud as possible, "I CHOOSE TO FIGHT!"

After returning to my car, I drove in a generally southerly direction for several hours, occasionally stopping to stretch my legs or grab something to drink or eat. Along the way, I decided I needed at least some plan to set me on a path to whatever the wind blows my way. I decided I would travel in a clockwise direction around the country. I would visit all the provinces and try to experience everything I could about the place.

I would not set a timeline or any plans. I would go and be there, learn what was special, and teach myself how to live once again. Of course, as Sophie had told me, Drink the wine! But maybe not so excessively as in the past weeks. I was determined not to let the prior weeks, heck, years! Set the tone for my journey.

Chapter 4

It was my third night on the road after I had left that mountain precipice and started towards the sea. I had never been to Venice but had heard many tales of its romance. However, at this time, I was less concerned with romance and more interested in finding a place to stay and adventure from. I called ahead and found a small room for a couple of days, just east of the city center in the village north of Venice. I had read online that there were many wineries in the area, so after checking in at the hotel, I decided to take Sophie's advice and venture out and see what I could find if I had only known what would happen next, and how it would change everything for me.

Though it was early afternoon, I decided to trek a little out of town to a local winery that the concierge had told me about. He said it was a regional family vineyard a bit off the typical tourist's path. He drew me a crude map and told me it would take me an hour or more to get there, but the winery stayed open until 5 pm for a few more weeks, as we were coming to the end of the harvest season.

So, I took the map from him and jumped in my car. She fired up like she knew something was about to happen, something of great importance. She always sounded amazing, but the way she started at the hotel's entrance was different. It was like she was a fire-breathing dragon and was ready to take flight at my command. I gently nudged the gearbox into first gear, and as I let out the clutch, the engine roared to life like never before. The screeching tires and the rumble of the engine as I pulled away only sent my senses into overdrive.

I quickly started shifting the dragon from first into second, third, and fourth, each time winding the engines up so loud she sounded like a fire-breathing dragon. I was so caught up in all the sensations that I was not thinking about where I was and who, if anyone, was watching. I hadn't gone three kilometers before local police caught up to me with his siren blazing.

I pulled my fiery beast to the side of the roadway; as he approached the car, I started getting all my paperwork out. I had gotten my Italian driver's license, so I was prepared to be fined or jailed. Of course, I spoke barely a word of Italian, but I understood enough that I needed to slow down. He graciously let me go. I think the dragon convinced him to let me go without making me pay that fine, but now I was behind schedule. As the officer turned around and headed back into town, I refreshed my memory with the map and swiftly nudged my dragon into our flight.

Two hours later, after three wrong turns and my aforementioned run-in with the police, I finally found the place. When I pulled into the drive, I noticed I was the only car there. I was hoping they had not already closed. I quickly got out of the car and could see a young lady inside through the open window. She looked to be cleaning glasses, so I assumed they were still open and proceeded to walk in the door.

Upon entering the room, which was quite large, I approached the young woman who looked to be in her mid-to-late 30s. She was polite and asked me how she could help. She had this lovely lilt to her voice. I think I froze. I had heard this kind of lilt before, but not wanting to relive that past, I brushed the feeling aside and asked her if I could get a tour and taste the wines.

She smiled and informed me that it was too late for a tour as she was closing, but if I wanted to sit at the far table in the back, she would gladly bring me a sample of their wines. I graciously accepted her offer, knowing she didn't have to since they were closing.

I quietly strolled through the vast room, which I now realized was very old and had many beautiful tapestries and paintings adorning its walls. As I settled into a chair facing out the windows and doors to the west, she closed the front door from which I had entered and locked it. She then proceeded to pick up a couple of glasses and a bottle of wine and came to the table. After sitting to my left so she could look out over the vineyard, she poured us a glass. It was a little informal but charming at the same time. I asked her if I was the only customer today; she gently nodded as she sipped the wine. She was so quiet you could have heard a mouse walk across the room. I followed suit and sipped the glass she had poured for me.

We sat in silence for a while. I noticed that her glass was almost empty and asked if I could pour her another glass. She nodded, accepting my offer; as I poured the wine, she asked me, "Do you like the view?"

I had spent most of the last twenty minutes looking at her. She had this mysterious look about her, alluring and sophisticated, but there was more to her story. By this time, I had remembered her voice and could not help but think of Francesca. It wasn't the same voice, but the lilt was, and the way she could stare at you and yet somehow look right through you simultaneously was utterly captivating. I struggled to answer her question, "Yes, the view is captivating."

She asked me if I preferred the setting sun or the morning sun. Of course, trying to be suave, I said, "It depends on who I am with."

She laughed. "I should have known you weren't watching the sunset."

I grinned sheepishly, as I was somewhat embarrassed now. She told me to pour myself another glass, relax, and soak up the moment. I did as I was told and sipped my wine while sitting peacefully, soaking up the moment. Occasionally, I would refill her glass, and she would nod for me to do the same with mine. It seemed the sunset would last forever, yet it was over in a fleeting moment.

She got up promptly and asked if I wanted something to eat. I was starved as I had not eaten since the cafe early that morning. She walked towards the serving room where she was prior. I couldn't help but watch her move. I don't know if it was the wine or the atmosphere, but she had the most wondrous walk. The curves of her hips and her tiny waist made for a perfect hourglass. She glanced back and laughed at me; she obviously could tell I was watching.

As she returned, I quickly shuffled myself to face her more as the sun had finished setting. She brought a small tray with some cheese, bread, and prosciutto. She also got another bottle of wine. Now, I like wine, but I am a two-bottle-a-week kind of wine drinker, and after drinking too much a few weeks before, I wondered if I was cut out for this.

She told me to finish my glass before she poured the new wine. I quickly drank the final sip from the glass. She filled it with water, then walked out the patio doors and poured it out into a pot of flowers. She asked if I would prefer to sit outside with the stars rather than in this dusty old room.

"Of course," I said, "let me get the tray." As I walked out, she took the tray from me and placed it at a two-person table next to a small fountain. She poured us some of the wine and sat across from me.

"*So, what's your story... How did you end up here?*"

"Well, I am from America."

She laughed again. "*Yeah, tell me something that is not obvious to everyone. Let me guess: You have recently divorced and are trying to find the love of your life. Heard it a thousand times.*"

She gave me this sharp look with almost a hint of anger. I quickly told her, "No, I am not recently divorced, well, at least not in the way you mean. I have a few ex-wives, but that was many years ago. I just needed a change in my life."

I started telling her how I had worked most of my life to provide for others and how that left me feeling empty and hollow. It was shocking, as I had hardly told myself many of these thoughts. She sat and drank her wine while sampling some of the cheese she had brought out earlier.

As I finished my tale, she asked, "*Well, I get who you are and where you are from, but you still have not told me why you are here, here in my winery, in my village.*"

I asked if I could have another glass. By this time, I was very relaxed, and the wine was certainly adding to this feeling. I could not stop watching her drink her wine. As the red juice touched her ruby red lips, they connected, like her lips were the wine and the wine was her lips. It was like if I sipped my wine while she was sipping hers, I could feel her lips against mine.

It was all very intoxicating, but I knew I needed to be honest with myself. She was much younger than I, and there was no way she would have been attracted to me, but I couldn't help myself. My eyes could not stop staring at her lips. It was like time had come to a stopping point, and there was nothing in the world except the two of us and her lovely lips. She put her glass down.

"*Think you need to pour us both another, judging by how you're looking at my lips.*" I once again stammered to regain my composure; *what was wrong with me?* I never act this way. But I did as she requested and told her I found my first, perhaps only true, love many years ago in Italy. She asked me what had become of her, and I told her about the tragedy. She said she was sorry for my loss but was sure she was not the only person for me. She said, "We all have multiple people we love and desire. You need to find yourself before you can be found by someone else."

That was so true; I no longer knew who I was. I had become a slave to my job and to the people who I supported, and I had never made time for myself. Sure, I bought myself toys, cars, boats, and houses, but the sad truth was they were all empty vessels to convince myself I was living a life. Her words pierced me like a dagger through the heart. I got reticent for a bit as I sipped the wine and stared up at the stars. It had been many years since I had taken the time to look at them. They were so spectacular that crisp autumn evening.

After she finished the cheese and bread, she told me to finish my wine, as she needed to get home. After I took my final sip, I quickly helped clean up the table and repositioned the chairs so they would be ready for tomorrow. As I returned to the front door, she yelled at me, "*Stop, please.*" I turned around and asked her, "Is everything alright?"

"No," she replied, "*I forgot I was supposed to ride home with one of the other workers this evening; I don't have a ride.*"

I quickly offered to give her a ride home if that would help. She stopped and stared at me.

"You're not some sort of criminal; you are not running from the police in America, are you?"

I told her I was not, but she could drive if she would prefer, as I honestly had no idea where I was. She said, "*Really, I can drive your car, THAT car?*"

"Of course you can; it is just a car."

It's funny how, for years, I would never let others drive my exotic cars, but now it was *just* a car.

Chapter 5

After I helped her mop the floors and clean off the bar, we got in the car. I realized I had never asked her for her name.

"Hey, can I ask what your name is, dear?"

"*Alessandra, but my friends call me Lexi. May I get to know yours?*"

"Of course; I am Nathaniel, but most people call me Nathan." She started up the car, and you could see the anticipation on her face. It was now late evening, and I had agreed to drop her off before returning to my hotel.

"*Hey, Nathan...LOL, it feels funny calling you that... Where are you staying?*"

"A hotel in the village just north of Venice."

"*WHAT? That is two hours from here, and you have drunk too much wine for that trip. Shit, what are we going to do...*"

As she pondered, I stupidly responded, "Well, I could always stay at your place." Oh, the look she gave me is something I will never forget.

"*Are you crazy or just that drunk? Don't get me wrong; I am flattered, but Nathan, you're way too old for me. I would break you in half if I took you to my bed.*"

I just sat there, embarrassed at what I had said and even more so at what I had implied. What was I thinking? Get a grip, man, and stop being an idiot! I would have been fine if I could have crawled into a hole somewhere and disappeared.

"*Ged... Hey, listen, I have a friend with a hotel in my village. I can get you a room there, and tomorrow, you can get yourself back. Does that work for you?*"

Of course, I would say yes to anything by this time, even if it was throwing me off a cliff and taking the car. I just needed to save what little dignity I had left.

As she pulled out of the winery, she looked over at me. She could see I was shaken by what I had said and done. She gently put her hand on my leg and said, "*Listen, you're a nice man, and maybe if you were a few years younger, but that's not where we are now. You are very handsome, and I am sure some lady will gladly take you to her bed, but why don't you fix yourself before you break someone else?*"

She was right. I needed to figure some stuff out in my head if I was ever going to be able to find a new life, a new love. I told her I appreciated her kindness and that she had been a lovely date, even though it was not a date. It was the first one I had been on in several years. She laughed. "Okay, we will call it a date. I suppose that means you are going to be wanting a kiss…" I decided to laugh, as I was unsure of the correct answer.

When we got to the hotel, it was small and charming, and she pulled the car around to the back where the owners parked. She told me the car would be safe back here and that she only lived a few blocks away in a little villa. I asked her if she would mind if I walked her to her place so I could try and be a gentleman, even though I had behaved so poorly before.

She agreed, and we began to walk. Before we left, she gave me the hotel's address and phone number in case I got lost. We walked quietly in the evening breeze. It was a chilling breeze, so I removed my jacket and gently placed it on her shoulders to warm her up. As I put the jacket on her, I noticed she had a tattoo I had not seen before, probably because I was too busy looking at her lips and hips.

After I slipped the jacket on her, she thanked me as we continued to walk. After about 15 minutes, we got to her place. She told me it had been fun, and she did enjoy my company, then leaned in and kissed me. I wanted to kiss her back so badly, but I knew better. I told her I had a fantastic time and hoped our paths might cross again someday.

She smiled. "You never can tell. For some reason, fate brought you to my winery. We shall see if fate brings us together again one day." With that, she opened the gate and walked in. I waved as she disappeared through the door.

On returning to the hotel, I realized I had left my jacket with her, but I didn't care. I considered it a souvenir she might have wanted to keep to remember me. The hotel was quaint but very friendly. They had left me an envelope at the front desk with my keys in it. After grabbing my day bag from the car, I went to my room, showered, and drifted off to sleep. All I could dream of was her wine-soaked lips, wondering if they tasted as divine as they looked. I could even smell her hair, as I had caught just a brief wisp of it when she had leaned in to kiss me. The fragrance of roses had been gently kissed by the sun after a spring rain.

Chapter 6

As I arose the following day, I felt a new calm. I was not rushed to be somewhere or do something like I had been for as long as I could remember. I packed my day bag, what little there was, and went down to pay the clerk. She said they had not charged me for the room as I was Lexi's friend. Right, I am Lexi's friend. Thank you so much.

I decided to toss my bag in the car and walk to see if I could find a local café for a coffee and a pastry. I saw one a few blocks down the path; it was small but had a few tables outside where I could sit and enjoy the morning. It was a cool morning, but not so cold that I missed my jacket. I was kind of glad Alessandra had decided to keep it, whether intentionally or not. It gave me some sense of satisfaction, knowing that a part of me was with her, as odd as that sounds.

After ordering my coffee and pastry, I stepped outside to sit. The kind clerk said she would bring it to me once it was ready. While I waited, I pulled out my journal. As I started writing about the prior day, my mind started swirling with all the senses and feelings I had experienced with Alessandra. I preferred her real name because it sounded more beautiful than just Lexi. Soon, the clerk came out with my cafe and pastry and placed them on the table. She asked me if I was a writer. I told her no; I was keeping a journal of my travels and experiences. She smiled. "Maybe someday you will make it into a book and include me in it."

"Of course," I said. She smiled and wished me a good day.

As I returned to my journal, the chair across from me was suddenly pulled out, and someone sat down. I was not from the area, so I decided to keep writing and not disturb them. After a few seconds, she flicked my journal with her long fingernails. I know those fingernails; they were the ones wrapped around the stem of the wine glass that was connected to those amazing lips.

I looked up and shouted, "Alessandra, you are here!"

She smiled. "*Shhh...keep it down. We like to be quiet here in the morning.*"

I apologized, "I didn't mean to be so gleeful, but it just sprang out."

She gave me that soft smile, "*I think you left your jacket with me, or should I say on me, last night.*"

I laughed, "Oh, you noticed!"

She let out a big laugh and quickly covered her mouth, "*Oh, my. You are incurable.*"

"What do you mean incurable?"

"*You have been bitten.*"

Okay, this was the second time I had heard the word *bitten.*

"What do you mean I have been bitten?"

"*I mean that if I told you I slept naked in your jacket last night, you would have a heart attack right here, in this café.*"

I didn't know what to say; the mental picture of her rolling around in her bed with nothing on but my jacket was more vivid than any erotic dream I had ever had before. I eventually said, "Never hurts to have a dream now, does it?"

She just smiled. A few minutes later, the clerk came out. "Hey Lexi, here is your morning cafe. You know this cutie?" pointing in my direction.

"*Yes, and he is trouble. He is from America and trying to find himself.*"

The clerk laughed, "Oh, a lost man looking for love."

Alessandra nodded and giggled at the same time. As the clerk walked away, she whispered something in Alessandra's ear, though I don't know what it was. I was hoping it was not about the reaction I had from the comment Alessandra had made about my jacket and her nakedness rolling around in it.

After a small chitchat, she asked me if I knew where I was and where I was heading next.

"Funny you should ask; I am not so sure now. Yesterday, I knew exactly what I was doing, but today. I think I will let fate take the wheel."

She smiled back, "*Well, fate brought you to my winery yesterday and my favorite café today. Seems like fate has something to say about all of this.*" I could not disagree; she was right: two chance meetings in such a short timeframe. I asked her, "Would you have time to show me around the village and maybe some of the countryside?" She pondered for a bit, not responding, then, "*Sure, but you have to let me drive.*"

"Gladly, as I would not know where we were going, anyways." We finished up our cafe and walked towards the hotel where my car was.

As we began walking, she asked me about my religious beliefs. I told her, "I guess you could say I am faithless, but you could not call me fate less. Love, yes, love is good enough for me."

She stopped. "*What kind of fucked-up answer is that?*"

I explained that the only thing I truly believed in was the love that fate hopefully would bring me. She again laughed at me, "*You have a funny way of thinking.*"

"What do you mean?"

"*You are so all business, all logical, but then you come up with these deep philosophical answers. I think you must have been a poet in a prior life, who knows, maybe even from Italy.*"

Her words struck me like a hammer on an anvil. I fell to the ground... I realized I had lived a fallacy; I had always focused on making logical and reasoned decisions. But in doing so, I had silenced, even buried, my emotions. I had never come to terms with the things from my past. I had pushed them aside and ignored them, telling myself I was doing the right thing. I had justified this compartmentalization to the point where I had forgotten how to do anything more than pretend to care about others.

As I sat on the path, I was reminded of who I was as a young man. I loved music and poetry and poured my soul into it, but when I fled home from years of confusion and pain, I forced myself into the character I had become. A practitioner of logic and reason, but one without heart, no soul, just an empty vessel. It scared Alessandra. I think she thought I was having a heart attack or something. She asked me, "Are you okay? Do I need to take you to a doctor?"

You could see the genuine concern on her face. I assured her I was perfectly fine, maybe even better than fine. It was like a set of shackles had been cut from my legs after long years of wearing them. I told her I needed to share something with someone but probably needed some wine to say to it.

"*Oh,*"—with a puzzled look—"Yes, please. This is very intense but good. All will be for the best. Please, allow me this one request."

She stood over me for a moment. “Okay, let us get the car. We can head back to the winery. We are closed today, as it is Wednesday, so nobody will be there, and there is certainly plenty of wine.”

Chapter 7

She remained quiet as we drove to the winery, occasionally glancing in my direction to ensure I was okay. She asked, "Please, tell me, I am worried…what happened back there? You turned almost grey as you collapsed to the ground."

I could tell she was apprehensive about what happened. It is hard to talk about this, as I have only now realized what I have been hiding from. It had been pushed deep within my heart and shut off from everyone, even myself.

"Okay, you can tell me, please. I want to help," she said as she drove through the countryside. I can still remember the smell of the air and how the sun felt on my face. I relaxed into the seat, took a deep breath, and then started my tale by sharing about Francesca, how we met, and that first trip to Italy. How when I returned home from that fateful trip, I continued to correspond with her. We wrote many letters back and forth. She started including vivid details of her passion for being with me, as I would write back to her with the same love and passion. It would take weeks for the letters to go back and forth, and the anticipation was sometimes unbearable. After a few months, my mother, with whom I had a difficult relationship ship, convinced me to move back in with her, as I was tired of not having a place to call home. After I moved in, she became very suspicious of the letters.

One day, she broke into my chest and took them. I was a young man, and she was in tears when I got home that evening. 'How could you?' she screamed at me. 'How could you?'

It was confusing as I did not know what she was referring to. Then, on the table in front of her, under the bottles of wine she had drank, I saw my letters from Francesca. She had read them all. I was horrified; this was like my journal, a diary. She got up, looked at me, and screamed, 'If you are good enough to love her, why don't you love me?' Then, pulling out a knife, she threatened to kill herself if I didn't love her. It was terrifying.

In a fit of fury, Alessandra abruptly stopped the car, throwing me into the dash and almost breaking my nose. "*WHAT THE FUCK!*" she screamed at the top of her lungs. "*You are telling me she threatened to kill herself if you didn't love her?*" She sat there, grasping for the correct response, but words seemed to fail her at that moment.

Sadly, it was all so confusing and frankly terrifying, and she was so upset and angry I didn't know what to think. I paused as I didn't know what else to say. After a few moments and more expletives, she slammed the car into gear and tore off toward the winery. She said, "*I will need some wine before I hear more of this story.*"

I was petrified; what was she thinking? What was I thinking? Had I made some huge mistake so many years ago? Oh, what cascade of events had I triggered? We spoke not a word during the next fifteen minutes, other than the occasional expletive she would shout out randomly. As we pulled into the winery, she looked at me. "We need a drink, and we need it now!"

Who was I to argue? My soul was torn into pieces, pieces that had never been truly mended. She threw the door open to the winery, grabbed not one but two bottles of wine, told me to grab the glasses, and that she would be in the garden. The bottles were on the counter, but the glasses were behind the bar, so I had to go behind the counter to get them. As she stormed off with the wine, she kept exclaiming some expletive every four or five steps.

Soon, she was out in the garden. I nervously found the nice glasses we had used the night before. There were hundreds of regular ones but a few nice ones, so it took me a few minutes. I put them on the counter and paused a moment to try and process everything that had happened—not just so many years ago but also what had just happened today.

After a moment, I composed myself, picked up the glasses, and walked out to the garden. When I arrived, Alessandra had opened the first bottle already and was drinking straight from it. I put down the glasses and asked if I could pour her a glass.

"*Sure, but open the other bottle and pour from it. This one will be empty soon enough.*"

Sure enough, the bottle she had in her hand was almost empty. I had been getting the glasses for a few minutes but didn't think it had been that long. I could see she was struggling to process all I had shared, but I knew I needed to let her take the next step if the conversation would continue.

Sitting in the garden, we drank our wine and remained quiet for the longest time. After a while, she stopped swearing and turned to me. "*What did you do?*" I sat for a moment, not even sure how I had responded. I mean, I knew I had fled but was not sure how to explain it all. I started again,

"Well, honestly, I was petrified. She was very drunk and distraught. I obviously didn't want her to hurt herself. But I wanted my letters from Francesca back. I reached for the letters, and she lunged towards me to keep me from them. At first, she missed again and then again, but on the third time, as I was grabbing for the remaining letters, she caught me with the knife. It went deep in my leg, and I screamed out in pain. She quickly froze as she realized what had happened, then pulled it out, but instead of being concerned, she just screamed:"

'This is what you have done to me!' she screamed.

Continuing, "After that, she ran to her bedroom and slammed the door. I grabbed a towel and put pressure on my leg to try and stop the bleeding, but it was flowing too much. I went to my room and got a belt. I had taken a life-saving class to be a beach lifeguard, so I knew I needed to make a tourniquet. I quickly found a belt and got the blood flow to stop mostly. I grabbed a few things and my letters and fled. As I descended the stairs in the apartment complex, a neighbor saw me. She could see the blood running down my leg. She was a nurse and helped me in her apartment. She ran down the hall and came back with a medical bag. She said, 'I shouldn't do this, but you won't make it to the hospital. You are losing too much blood. She hit an artery, and I have to clamp it and stitch it, or you are going to die! Do you understand?' I nodded that I understood. She apologized that she had no painkillers and gave me some wooden kitchen utensils to bite and a pillow to hold onto. Both her daughters jumped out of bed and ran in to help. Everything started turning black and white, and all I can remember is her saying, 'Shit, he might bleed out! Girls, hold him down.' Sometime later, I woke up in one of their beds in intense pain. As I groaned from the pain, she told me I was going to be okay, but I needed to be still. For the next couple of days, I hid in their apartment while she and her daughters nursed me back to health."

Suddenly, Alessandra interrupted, "*FUCK! First, she tries to threaten to kill herself, and then she almost kills you... Did you call the police?*"

I told her that if we had called the police, they would have taken my mother to jail for sure, but they would have also taken the lady who saved my life to jail for illegally practicing medicine. It was a fucked-up situation.

Alessandra nodded. "*Yes, I can understand that, but that is a fucked-up situation for sure.*"

I picked up the story about a week later, finally being able to walk without mind-numbing pain. The lady who helped me asked, '*What are you going to do?*' I thought to myself, what am I going to do? It was an honest question. I had a job working on a boat and another at a local market, but where would I sleep? Where would I take a shower? Holy crap, what am I going to do?

Later that day, I snuck into my mother's place while she had gone to work and got all things. Then, I drove to a local music shop and made a deal to sell it all to them. It broke my soul to sell what had brought me to Francesca. Without those, I would have never met her; I would never be happy without her. At least, at that time, that is how I felt. With the money I got, I drove to the small beach town and found a hotel I could rent monthly. They were used to renting to young people for the summer, and I had cash, so they did not ask any questions. I moved into the hotel. Later that first night, I realized I was on my own; I would have nobody except myself to take care of me. There would be no more food on the table, no more clothes in the closet, and nobody to take care of me when I got sick. Something died inside me at that moment. I told myself it was time for me to grow up, like a ritual, from being a child to being a man. I referred to it as my Passing into Manhood.

Chapter 8

After I finished, we sat in silence together for some time. Then Alessandra got up and returned to the winery with a third and fourth bottle of wine. I looked at her and asked, "Are you okay? I am sorry I burdened you with this. It was never my intention to cause you any pain."

She leaned in, hugged me, and said, "*It will be okay.*" Then she poured us both more wine. We sat and drank for many more hours, doing our best to make a joke or two, but there was no way to avoid what had happened. Once again that evening, we shared a cheese and bread plate and continued to talk. After we finished, she got up and said, "*Well, we are both too drunk to drive anywhere, so we will have to stay here.*"

"Here!" I exclaimed. "In the garden?"

"*No, silly, we have a honeymoon suite we rent that is over the main winery building. But don't get any ideas. You get the couch. You know we are not getting married tonight.*" She laughed as she started to walk off. "*Follow me.*" It was a lovely suite with a nice bath and shower. We agreed I would take the couch, as she had already announced that earlier, and we would take turns getting cleaned up. She went first and took her shower. When she emerged, she was wearing nothing but a robe, her makeup was gone, and her hair was wet. I had never seen anything as beautiful.

I remember thinking there are moments in life that will never escape you, and this was one of those. She excused herself to her room, and I then cleaned myself up. She had left me a robe as well. When I walked out, she had kindly placed a blanket and a pillow on the couch for me. As I lay on the sofa, I could not get rid of the image of her walking out in the robe. It was the first time I could remember being inspired in a very long time. I soon fell asleep.

The following day was warm and sunny. We both got up, dressed and decided we needed to get to a café and get something to drink and eat. We cleaned up the Non-Honeymoon suite, as I called it, much to Alessandra's amusement. She always said she was probably the only girl to ever sleep in that room that didn't get blissfully fucked. Once we got to the café, we discussed what to do next. It was like she had decided to be my tour guide.

Of course, I was not disappointed with this arrangement; she was such a delight to be with. As we talked, we decided she would take me into Venice, as I had never been, and show me what most people don't get to see. With that plan, we took to the road.

As we were heading to Venice, Alessandra looked at me, "*Crap, we didn't pack anything, and your suitcase is still at your hotel.*" I told her, "Don't worry about it. I need to leave the past in the past, and I would be honored if you would allow me to show you a few kindnesses for all you have done for me." She reluctantly agreed, reminding me, "*We are NOT getting married or anything near that, so get those thoughts out of your mind!*"

There was always this exciting glint in her eyes. Every time she said it, she changed the tone ever so slightly. Maybe it was just my wishful thinking, but I decided I must hold on to what fate brings me.

When we reached Venice, she called a local hotel she knew and arranged for a two-room suite, with the exact agreement of the couch for me for the next three nights. She insisted it would take at least that long to truly appreciate and absorb Venice's atmosphere. I happily agreed. This was a complete adventure; I had no idea where I would be today, much less tomorrow. And then there were her lips and hips; I found myself always walking behind her to watch them gently pivot from side to side, like a clock that kept perfect time with the beat of my heart. If she walked faster, my heart would beat faster, and if she walked slower, so did the beating of my heart. I could not shake the sensation, no matter how hard I tried to push it out of my mind. I would daydream like a schoolboy sitting next to a girl for the first time and seeing her legs under the desk.

After we checked in at the hotel, we decided we needed to get some food and maybe some wine. She took me to this quiet place off the beaten path. She ordered us a local specialty; it was a very Venetian meal, as she put it. When they brought it to the table, it was delicious, and we ate our meals. She told me tales of her childhood home and how her family had been in the winery business for generations, but the winery was her grandfather's brother, and she felt lucky to be part of it. Her father seemed to have had a more difficult time. She explained they were always getting by but insisted her parents loved her and her brothers very much. I could tell she was holding back; there was some painful memory she was unwilling or incapable of talking about. I knew it was not my place to ask more, as I had always hated it when people wanted to know about my past.

After we finished, she recommended we take a walk through the city and see what direction fate would lead us. She very much liked to let fate run its course. As we walked, the night got colder, with damp air coming in from the sea. I took my coat that she had worn a few nights prior and covered her shoulders. She acknowledged the warmth it brought her and walked beside me to block the breeze from my now bare arms.

It was a sweet gesture, and she was right—I was freezing, but I would never show it. We walked and talked for hours, occasionally stopping for a glass of wine, and then we would be on our way to see what fate would bring our way. Around 2 am, I realized we needed to start at least thinking about getting back to the hotel; it was now cold, and I was without a jacket. She could see I was freezing, so she moved up next to me and put her arm around my shoulders so that we could share our one jacket.

As we walked back to the hotel, arm in arm, I could not help myself. Every time she took a step, her right breast would brush against my left arm. She was wearing a thin cashmere sweater top, and her nipples were very erect from the cold. But in my mind, I was hoping, maybe even praying, though I don't pray, that perhaps it was me causing this reaction.

When we got to the hotel, we headed to the room. She jumped into the shower almost as soon as she cleared the door's threshold. After what seemed an eternity, she opened the door to the bath. The steam rolled out of the room. She looked at me. "*Oh no, you are freezing! Get in there and warm up.*"

I jumped up and shuffled to the bath. She had left the shower on, but when I got in, my skin was so cold that I felt like pieces of molten fire were pelting me. I must have screamed as she came running in to make sure I was okay. And there I was, butt-ass naked, standing in the shower, looking at her with her robe wide open. I became instantly aroused at the sight of her.

Her wet hair was draped across her breasts, with the nipples protruding through her thick, luscious dark hair. They moved up and down as she struggled to catch her breath after running into the bath. As my eyes moved down her torso, I could see how lovely her waist was and then below, her womanly fruit. She looked at me.

"*I can see you are not hurt, judging by that.*" She had noticed what was now my fully aroused. I started to reach for a towel to cover myself. "*Stop that!*" she exclaimed. "*What I have seen, I have seen; nothing is going to change that, just like what you have seen, you have seen. But that is your problem, not mine. Good luck getting to sleep tonight.*" Then she turned, dropped her robe to the floor, and walked out the door but not closing it.

Then she came back in. "*Oh, excuse me, I dropped my robe!*" Turning her bum to me, showing me her wonderfully sexy body. Then, walking out, she proceeded to her room and closed the door behind her. I finished my shower, put on my robe, and tried not to think about it. I went to the couch where, once again, she had kindly put out a blanket and pillow. I finally drifted off to sleep, but the images of her danced in my mind all night.

The next morning, I found her standing over me with a look of satisfaction and disgust. I wondered what she was thinking. "*Look at yourself. What are you going to do about that thing? You cannot go out publicly with that thing sticking out everywhere, all day.*"

Then, with her finger, she pointed at my blanket. I had not even noticed, as the last couple of mornings had been the same way, but I had been able to get up and compose myself before she saw it. Then, with a quick smack of her hand, she slapped me across the face. It hurt like hell, but it worked. As she turned, she commented, "*What have I let fate get me into now!*"

Once we got dressed, we left the hotel and walked towards the Piazza San Marco. There was a Basilica she said we needed to see. Along the way, we grabbed a cafe and decided we would spend the afternoon getting some new clothes, as we were on day three of these clothes. I think we were both no longer wearing undergarments, as I could occasionally get a faint wisp of her feminine nectar. It was intoxicating, but I would never mention it as I would not have wanted to offend her.

After she gave me her custom tour of the piazza and the Basilica, we retreated to the shopping district, where we quickly resolved our clothing issues. She was a fan of nice clothes, and I was happy to indulge her desires. She got some tops, a few skirts, dresses, shoes, and a coat. She then took me to a custom Italian tailor and had him prepare some pants and shirts for me,

which she thought were more appropriate for a gentleman in Italy. She let me keep my cowboy hat but insisted I get a leather coats to wear. I convinced her she also needed to get a leather coat so we could match. She thought it was cute, so she indulged me and got the coat. We then returned to the hotel to drop off all our new clothes. Once we arrived, we both decided we needed to get out of our old clothes and put on some nicer things. She got in the shower first. Just as I heard the water come on, she walked out the door fully naked.
"*Shit, I forget I need some undergarments.*"

I assured her we would go as soon as we got cleaned up. With that, she turned around, revealing that fantastic bum, and got back in the shower, but this time, she left the door partially open. I started to think, was this fate giving me an invitation, or did the door just not latch? Though I wanted to do so badly, I decided to be prudent and not peek in the door. Once she finished and was dressed, I quickly did the same.

We quickly made haste to a ladies' lingerie store close to where we had been shopping earlier. She asked me to wait outside because she didn't want people to think I was creepy. I nodded and handed her some money to pay for what she needed as she quickly disappeared inside. About 30 minutes later, she emerged, stating, "*Okay, now I am finally appropriately a lady again.*" I laughed and told her she always was, and even if she wasn't, who cares? It is just the two of us on what now seems to be an adventure somewhere. We decided to get a quick meal that night, as we were both a bit tired from all the walking and the prior days. We had a nice plate of cheese and bread and an excellent wine bottle. I was once again mesmerized by how the color of the wine was perfectly shaded with the color of her lips. She must have seen me looking, who knows, maybe drooling…shit, I can't remember.

She stated, "*Hey, don't forget we aren't a couple. Just because you have seen my body doesn't mean you're going to enjoy its pleasures.*" I quickly looked down at my wine as she let out a howl, laughing at me so hard she could barely catch her breath. After she stopped laughing at me, she leaned over, kissed me, and told me, "Relax, live in the moment fate has brought us this far. Who knows where it will take us tomorrow?" I nodded, kissed her back, and finished my wine.

We soon retreated to the hotel, where we talked about nothing for the longest time, but the conversation with her was always easy. Soon, she got up, kissed me again, and said goodnight. I kissed her back and said, "Sweet dreams, *Mia Bella.*" She turned and looked at me. "*So, you think I am beautiful?*" Then she disappeared into her room, and I drifted off to sleep.

Chapter 9

The next morning, we decided to head down to the sea and ride a gondola through the canals. As she said, "*It is a must; you have not been to Venice unless you ride in a gondola.*" I laughed, "Okay, let's do it. No, wait!" She stopped and looked at me. "*What?*" Smiling at her, "I thought you had to ride on a gondola with your lover while being serenaded." She smiled back, "*Well, we are not there, but I am happy to be serenaded next to you today.*"

So off we headed out, and as usual, grabbed a cafe and pastry along the way. We didn't reach the canals until noon as we got distracted. We decided to pick up a bottle of white wine on the way. We soon found ourselves in the gondola. When I sat down, I realized she could only sit in front of me, leaning back on me as the gondola was not wide enough for us to sit side by side. She laughed and said, "*Sit down, you silly fool!*"

It had become her new pet name for me. Once I was seated, she stepped in and gently fell back into my arms. The gondolier started our journey as we started drinking the wine. Soon, he began singing about lovers and the passion of their desires. Between the smell of her hair wafting across my face, the wine, and the song, I was soon in a complete trance.

She leaned forward and tickled my ribs to break me out of my trance. As I began to laugh, I spilled my wine. She laughed out loud, "*Now look at you and your pants. Great, I guess this makes me look like your lover now. Who would have thought fate would have done this to me?*" She poured me another glass as we continued our journey through the canals.

As the afternoon passed, I became completely intoxicated by everything about Alessandra. I could no longer kid myself; this was the same passion I had felt for Francesca many years before. She was so beautiful, like a Goddess with wings. She floats above me but just out of reach, making me want her even more. When the gondola came to rest, we quietly got out and went to the hotel. She insisted I change my pants before she would go to dinner with me.

I agreed and politely excused myself to get changed. When I was done, she excused herself into the bath for a few minutes. She came out and was beyond words, looking like a miracle had fallen into my life. I was shaking as she walked up to me and kissed me. "*It will be all okay; just be with me tonight.*" What did she mean to be with her? At dinner? For a walk? What did she mean? She took me to another one of her favorite spots, and once again, she ordered our meals. I had no idea what we were eating. I was utterly fixated on what she had whispered to me moments before. As I watched her drink the wine, I was consumed with a passion that had escaped my life for years. This was what life was all about.

As the dinner ended, I asked her if she would like to go for a walk. "*Is that really what you want to do?*" she asked. How was I to answer this? What did she want me to say? Whatever it was, I would say it. I could not contain myself. I reached out, grabbed her by her hand, and then quickly wrapped my other arm around her waist and pulled her to my lips. I kissed her with the passion that I had long forgotten I could have within me. I soon noticed she was kissing me back. Not aggressively, but certainly with intent.

We moved to the door stoop next to the restaurant and continued to kiss and caress each other's bodies. Our bodies seemed to merge as we playfully and passionately kissed one another. At that moment, I realized that she was a Goddess, and she had descended from the heavens to heal me from all the trauma I had been through. With apprehension, I led her back to the hotel, unsure what to expect…

Chapter 10

As we reached the rooms, she excused herself and pointed to her room. "*I will be in soon.*" It was all she said. Did she mean for me to go in and wait for her? If I went in, should I stay dressed, should I get undressed, should I get in bed… WHAT SHOULD I DO? I quickly decided I would grab a bottle of sparkling wine from the cooler in the room. I quickly found some glasses and brought them to her room. Just as I started to open the bottle, she walked in.

I could not think, move, or do anything at all. I was frozen in her beauty. She was the most divine thing I had ever seen. She was wearing a black bra that was both see-through and not see-through. It had lace around the edges, which only seemed to enhance the shape of her perfect breasts. As I stood there, she took the bottle from me, turning around to open it.

As she turned, I quickly noticed the black thong panties she was wearing that accentuated the shape of her hips with its high-cut V waist. It melted me to my soul. The thin string disappeared into her luscious bum and then reappeared just as it curved to go under her feminine fruit. As I grasped her, I heard the cork pop free from the bottle. She turned around and started pouring me a glass, then pouring herself one to match. I asked, "What should we toast to?"

"*To fate,*" she replied. I whispered in her ear, "Your loving touch has freed me from my prison." As I finished, I saw she was clutching at a choker around her neck. It was then that I saw the tears streaming from her face, matching those streaming from mine. I took our glasses and placed them gently on the table. I turned around and reached out my hand to her, where she slowly raised her to match mine.

We pulled towards each other and fell into a lover's embrace. I whispered to her, "Tonight may be but a fleeting moment, but the memory of this moment, of you and the love you have shown me, will remain with me forever." We fell into our first lover's embrace; it was beyond words to describe. It felt as though our blood was shared; as she breathed, I breathed, and she moved; I moved; it was something I had never experienced; it was divine, like the angel with wings had touched my heart and had started the path to mending my broken soul.

When we awoke, we were both still lost in the moment from what had transpired the night before. The room was in complete disarray as we had thrown caution to the wind. We both sat up and looked about the room. Alessandra looked at me and laughed. "*Well, it looks like I didn't break you in half after all. What did I do to fate to get myself in this mess?*"

It is all she said. I was unsure how to take this. Was she serious, perhaps feeling a sense of regret for what happened, or was she just being playful? As she got up and dragged the sheets off the bed, she walked to the bath. She turned around and looked at me. "*Stop looking at me that way.*"

"What way?" What was my face showing? I thought to myself. I was panicked. I had always been so composed, never really getting overly excited about anything. I guess it was part of my emotion suppression protocols, which I had imposed on myself so many years before.

"*You know what I mean. Wipe that ear-to-ear smile off your face; otherwise, I will have to come back and kiss you again.*"

"Oh, well, what would be so wrong with that?"

"*We must check out in 45 minutes; it's almost noon, you silly fool.*"

Shit, I had no idea how time had passed so fast but yet seemed to be frozen all at the same time. With that, she turned and got in the shower. I got myself up and composed our things, gathering them up so that when she was done, I could do the same, and we could get on the road to our next destination. Oh yeah, where were we going next?

We spent so much time wandering but have yet to discuss what was next. Would she want to continue our adventure, or did she need to return home to her village and continue with her life? The thought of her leaving me made me shudder with fear. No, I kept telling myself that she would certainly want to continue after last night.

But deep inside, I grew to fear this was just a moment for her; maybe she felt pity for me. Oh, jeez, what have I done? Did I make her feel obligated when buying all those clothes? I would never have done that; what have I done? Soon, she walked out and barked at me to get in there and get cleaned up as we had to get going.

I quickly disappeared behind the bathroom door and stood in shock. Was this happening? I got in the shower and cleaned myself up, but the shower pouring water on my head felt like the maelstrom raging in my heart. Once I got out, I told myself I would be respectful and gracious, and if she were ready to go home, I would gladly, with a smile, take her. I would be the consummate gentleman, no matter how much it hurts.

When I walked out, she was sitting on the couch I had spent so many nights sleeping on. She looked at the watch I had bought for her and tapped it with her finger. "*We got to go...*"

I grabbed our stuff, and we took off for the car. We chitchatted in the elevator to the garage but have yet to discuss what we will do next. Once we got to the car, I put our stuff in the boot. We had bought too much for such a small car, so I put our coats behind our seats. I then opened the driver's door and asked her to please drive.

I had decided this would be the quickest way to see her thinking. I would know this was just a fling for her if she turned for home. She thanked me. "*I cannot remember the last time I have had a gentleman open a door for me. And to think you always do it. Hmmm.*"

After she sat, I gently closed the door and walked to my door. It seemed like it took forever; the dread continued to build with every step. When I reached my door, I felt like I was carrying the world's weight on my shoulders and heart. I slowly got in the car and exhaled.

I must have been loud about it without realizing it. "*What's wrong with you, my silly fool?*" she asked. I didn't know how to start the conversation, what I was going to say to her, or what she was going to say to me. The anticipation of my certain doom was overwhelming. I finally just said, "I suppose I am taking you back to your village today?" with a certain amount of disdain and frustration. She looked over at me and smacked me so hard it brought blood to my mouth. I screamed in pain as I had not been hit that hard since I was in a schoolyard as a child. "*You think that I only fucked you for the hell of it? Is that what you think?*" in a booming voice that echoed throughout the garage. I tried my best to collect my thoughts, but before I could open my mouth, she started screaming at me with many Italian words, which I was sure were not kind-loving.

I quickly grabbed her hand with the most passion I could express; she instantly pulled it from me. I leaned over, grabbed her head, and kissed her as passionately as I could. I wanted to reassure her that I did not think any of that. And since I lacked the words to express it, I was only left with my lips. At first, she resisted, twisting her head back and forth so that I was unable to engage the kiss. Then, in a moment of panic, I whispered in her ear, "Kiss your silly fool, Mia Bella."

She immediately stopped screaming at me, quickly looking into my eyes with her stormy eyes. Then she grabbed the back of my head and pulled me into an aggressive but passionate kiss. We kissed for several minutes before our embrace was disrupted by a man who knocked on her car window to ask if she was okay. "Is this man bothering you?" he asked her.

"*No, officer, we just had our first Italian lover's quarrel.*" He quickly smiled, knowing something I did not.

With that, he excused himself; as she rolled her window up, she turned and looked at me. "*Listen, my fool, my darling fool. What happened last night was not a simple thing, but it was certainly something more than just a fuck.*"

I smiled and agreed. It had been something very unique, something I had honestly not felt emotionally before. She leaned back in her seat. "*Well, now that we are over that, where are we off to?*"

I looked at her and said, "The way out of this journey will be the first step into our next adventure"

"*What are you babbling about?*"

I told her the way out of Venice was the way into the next chapter of our adventure. "*So, by leaving, we are beginning all over again.*"

"Yes, exactly, but the destination is unknown." We both smiled.

Alessandra looked at me. "*Well, choose a direction, and we shall go. By the way, we can't go south without a boat, just in case you didn't know, silly fool,*" she laughed.

"True, and this is most decidedly not a boat. Let us go East and then turn south along the sea," I declared. And with that, she started our next adventure. I remember the sun on my face, the sun shining through her long, dark hair as we drove out of town. It was like some fantasy from a movie ending, but this was just the beginning. I decided that Venice was the prologue of our story. We had yet to get to our story's first chapter as I scribbled the prior days' events into my journal.

Alessandra looked over at me. "*You better say I am sexy in that book of yours.*"

I smiled. "Oh, I will say much more than that."

She howled with laughter, "*Just do not make me into some sort of, well, you know. Okay?*"

I looked at her. "*Il mio bellissimo angelo alato*. I would never speak of my angel in that fashion."

She smiled, "*What will fate bring us today?*" Then she gunned the gas as we were on our way once again.

The Road Runs Beneath

Our night has passed
Into the light of new day
The light of that day
Will pass into our night

With our feet
like our fortunes
We stand committed
We stand resolute

But the road runs beneath
The road runs beneath

Fate has watched us
Casting its gazed light
We stand in her darkness
But yet it is bright

To what awaits
Our fortune's unseen
We fill up our hopes
We fill up our dreams

But the road runs beneath
The road runs beneath

The darkness of fate's light
Be a beacon to our sight

But the road runs beneath
The road runs beneath

Interlude
Can I Burn My Ship?

Before leaving home, I had decided to start with a clean slate. The old proverbial 'burning the ships at the shore, making it impossible to sail home.' So, with that decision, I made the arrangements to start selling most of my things that were still back there. It was a long list, so I got a friend to help liquidate my estate. I was, however, very torn on whether to sell my home; I had spent so many years personally overseeing its growth.

When I first acquired the property, it was in complete disarray; I could even say it was virtually unlivable. But, after many years of effort, I had turned the place into a natural retreat. The views from the patios were terrific. I would sit every afternoon and watch the sunset over the hills surrounding the lake below. I was not directly on this lake but had easy enough access, though I seldom used it. But the brilliant sunsets were the hallmark event that tied me to this place.

I had come to think of it as my final resting place, the place I would spend my ending days. I had figured out where I wanted my ashes spread as my final resting spot. So, to sell this place, well, was I decided, outside the cards. However, that would mean I had left myself a life raft to return to my former existence, as I could no longer call it a life.

I have always told people that a life without risks is merely an existence without life. I was convinced that the risks I was taking would prove to others and myself that I was living an extraordinary life. The sad truth is that I had misinterpreted the meaning behind this dramatic statement. I had rested so much of my life upon its words. I always thought the risks it was referring to were those related to my business decisions or riding motorcycles in sandstorms, snow, tornadoes, or even worse. But now I realized the risks the poet was referring to be the risks of the heart—the willingness and ability to follow that fateful journey with no net to catch you.

In my business world, I had always had other options; we always had plan Bs, and our plan Bs had their plan Bs. But with the heart, there is no plan B; you must give your heart's contents, chaff, and grain together. Hoping, even praying, that those who would measure those contents would sift out the chaff and be able to keep the grain. To separate your flaws, failures, and frailties and somehow see the good parts of your soul, the things that make you human, loving, caring, and patient.

This was the risk I had never been able to take, not only with others but with myself. I realized that the person that needed to be able to do this sifting first was myself. I had to be able to take all my soul and accept those ugly, painful, and downright horrible things and still see the good, the passion, the love, and the spirit of whom I truly was. Until I could do that, I would be stuck on a wheel that spins round and round, sometimes fast and sometimes slow, but never touching the ground and allowing me to move forward.

Chapter 11

We raced like two rabbits across a vast grass field, searching for something while trying to evade the predators eagerly awaiting us. The day started a bit tumultuous, but once we got past the apprehension of the morning, we were in a joyful, even gleeful mood. We had decided to head down the coast of the Adriatic Sea and visit the small villages and, of course, wineries we came across. We had no destination; we would drive until we saw something and let fate lead us.

Around mid-afternoon, we found an open winery; as we had yet to eat, we decided to stop and sample the wine and get some food. It was a lovely vineyard; it was more coastal, and you could see the sea from their veranda and feel the sea breeze as it rushed up the hillside. Even though it was autumn, the middle of the day's sun could still burn bright, so the breeze was a refreshing reprieve. As we sat, sipped our wine, and snacked on our bread, fruit, and cheese tray, we spoke about the day and night before.

We laughed at the wine on my pants in the gondola on more than one occasion. Alessandra liked to tease me about my lack of control of my bodily functions. She found it a limitless fodder to embarrass and make me turn as red as the wine we were drinking. I was drawn to watching the red wine kiss her lips as usual. However, now, I realized the wine must be jealous of her lips; her lips were more intoxicating than the wine and much more flavorful. However, I must admit I was still envious of the wine as I was eager to taste them again.

Once we finished up our tray of food, I asked the waitress if we could have a bottle of wine and stroll the property as we needed to stretch our legs. She brought us a bottle and a blanket and told us there was a nice, secluded spot up the hill from the winery where you could see the entire coastline. I thanked her, paid our bill, and left her a nice tip. As we were about to start the trek up the hill, she whispered, "I wanted to let you know your car is parked outside the gates, so feel free to stay as long as you like. We close in two hours, but stay and enjoy, please."

I thanked her for the offer and suggestion and started our trek. As I carried the blanket, Alessandra took the wine; soon, our free hands were intertwined like the trellis of vines. We pushed and pulled on each other like school kids; occasionally, she would break free, run up the hill, and tease me about being old and slow. I constantly reminded her that the tortoise won the race, not the rabbit. She would smirk at me and race ahead.

I just maintained my pace as I could see we still had a way to go, and there was a significant climb we would need to make if we wanted to get to the top. By the time we reached the base of the final hill, she had worn herself out with the running ahead and taunting me routine, but she was a fighter and would never give up. Together, we made the modest climb to the top of the knoll. There was a lovely tree with some shade, so we laid out the blanket to enjoy the sun.

We could see all the surrounding areas and noticed that all the guests and most of the other cars at the winery had gone. Though the coast was to our East, we decided to face West and watch the setting sun. I backed up against the tree, and she fell into my arms. We opened the wine and sat peacefully, just soaking up the moment. Just about then, I could see she was hatching a plan. Alessandra had a bit of an irreverent streak in her that I adored.

I had spent so many years doing the right thing, so it was lovely to be with someone who would do the opposite—not criminal, mind you, but risky. "*Hey, I have an idea; since we are heading south and will certainly go to a beach along the way, I want to get rid of my tan lines.*"

"Okay," I responded, not sure what she was thinking. It was then she pulled off her top and removed her bra, then proceeded to do the same with her skirt and panties. She laid down on the blanket at my feet, sunning her Goddess-like body. I just sat there sipping my wine, completely enthralled with what I had found myself next to.

"*Hey, you going to join me down here?*" she chirped. "Sure." I began to reposition myself to lay beside her. I took my shirt off, a bit embarrassed as I was not a bodybuilder, though I was not a potbelly pig either. Once I got my shirt off, I started to lie down.

"*What are you doing?*"

"Laying down; why?"

"*No, you're not, this is a no-clothes zone; if you want to lay next to me, that is the price of admission.*" She laughed. I was honestly now really embarrassed. Not only had I not done anything like this since I was a kid, but after staring at her body for the last several minutes, I was more than aroused. But she insisted and started to tease me, "*Ah, is the schoolboy afraid of the girl with no clothes on?*" She just kept laughing and giggling. Eventually, I gave in and removed my shorts. "*Well, hello there,*" was the first thing she said. "Great, now you are going to tease me about being aroused after staring at you?"

"*No, no, quite the opposite.*" With that, she reached up and pulled me to the ground on top of her. She instantly began kissing me with those lips. We continued to frolic that afternoon and made passionate love under that tree on the knoll. As night came upon us, it was getting cold, so we got dressed and wrapped up in the blanket, which was a little wet and smelling of…well, sex. But we didn't care; we were letting fate have her way. "*Bet you never thought you would do that today,*" she smiled.

"What, make love to a Goddess?"

"*No, you fool, under the tree on the hill part of it.*"

"Honestly, I could have been anywhere. It was you I was with, and the surroundings were just the canvas on which I painted my passion for you." She turned a bit red. It was the first time she had ever blushed around me that I could remember.

"*Stop calling me a Goddess. I am not perfect, you know!*"

"I never said a Goddess was perfect; a Goddess is a divine creature that knows when to be good and when to be bad."

"*Haha, very funny, but I certainly can live up to that description; I can certainly be bad.*" She looked at me with a wild, almost carnal gaze. I pulled her to me and kissed her as I could not resist. She reciprocated with a bit more ferocity when she bit down on my lower lip and pulled away, causing it to bleed just a bit. But she kept kissing, and it was another one of those moments you will never forget. Until then, our passion had been feverish but more in loving nature; this was something else altogether. Once we got to the car, she found a hotel very close. "*We have somewhere to be and something to do.*"

What was she talking about? Should I be concerned? The last time I saw something like this was long ago with Francesca, but Alessandra was not Francesca. If Francesca was a lynx, then Alessandra was a full-on panther.

As she drove feverishly to the hotel, she looked over at me. "*Don't be worried; I won't bite, well, not too much,*" with an almost devilish laugh. It wasn't very comforting but exhilarating all at the same time. As we pulled into the hotel, she told me to get the keys and she would grab the stuff from the car. I was dutiful, hurried to the office, and handled the paperwork. She had reserved their only cottage, so by the time I got to the cottage, the bags were all on the porch with her standing next to them:

"*Open the door, you fool,*" she whispered. I could not open it fast enough; my anticipation of what was about to occur was full force. As the door opened, she grabbed a bag, but it was one I had not seen the day before. I wonder what is in that bag, I thought.

After I got all the bags into the room and closed the door, Alessandra asked me to pour some wine for us. I did as she requested and sat with both glasses on the couch, awaiting her arrival. When she emerged from the bath, I thought she might be dressed as she was the night before in Venice, but nope. I was dead wrong. She stepped out in a tight leather outfit. It had a zipper up the front that she had only zipped up to her navel.

Then, turning around and looking over her shoulder. "*You like?*"

Of course, she knew how to tease me. As she turned around, I could see the outfit was a single strap of leather that ran from her shoulder blade, disappearing in the crease of her buttocks; a few other strings like lace went around to attach to the front. "My God, look at you."

I sat staring at her. "*Well, you said a Goddess could be bad; you better prepare yourself for my bad.*" She rushed to the couch and tackled me like I was holding a bag of diamonds, and she wanted them. The rest of the night was a giant passion-filled blur; we exercised our passions on each other and together. When the night was done, we were both spent and completely exhausted. We decided to shower together to clean up and head off to bed. Of course, I would need to make the bed as the sheets, pillows, and blankets were everywhere except on the bed. "*So, you still think I am a Goddess?*"

"Most assuredly, I had only ever met one other woman who was so confident with her sexuality and desires, and you are that, times two."

"*Two, just two? Well, maybe we should get out of this shower right now and let me have my way with you some more.*"

"No, it was not a measurement like that. I stated that you are far more than anything I could have dreamed and that there is nothing to compare you to."

"*Good, you almost ruined the moment, silly fool!*" she laughed. We finished the shower, straightened up the bed, and held each other tightly as we fell asleep.

The following day, the shadows found us. Before we even had gotten out of bed, her phone started buzzing. At first, she ignored it, but it kept going off every few minutes. She thought maybe she had turned an alarm on by accident, but that would not be the case. Her mother texted her that she needed to call home immediately. She jumped out of bed, ran into the bath, and called her mother. Several minutes later, she came out; she was visibly upset and had been crying. She crawled back into bed. "*Please, just hold me,*" was all she said. I held her with the most tender arms I could. I decided I dare not ask, that she would tell me when she was ready.

As she sat there crying in my arms, I felt so helpless. Not only did I not know what was wrong, but I also needed to figure out how I would help. After an hour or even more, she sat up and faced me. "*Please don't be mad. Please promise me you won't be mad.*"

"Of course, I won't be mad." I could never be mad at her; it was just impossible.

"*I...I...have to go home.*"

"Okay, we will leave immediately."

I got up and started putting our things together. "You are going to take me?"

"*My God, of course, I am; I love you.*" Shit, I said it…Crap…Now was not the time to say that… "I am sorry. I should have never said that; I am so" Before I could get the words out of my mouth, she jumped out of the bed, wrapped her arms around my neck, and hugged me as she had never hugged me before. "*Shhh, just shut up, you fool; if you have not figured it out yet, I am falling in love with you as well.*" I fell to my knees, dropping to hers she met me. "I don't know what to say." I gently whispered to her.

"*I know,*" is all she said. "*Will you come home with me and help me bury my father?*" Holding her close, "I am so sorry. I have no words to express my sorrow for your loss. I will always be there for you; you never have to ask." She hugged me back, kissed me, and whispered, "*Thank you.*"

We quickly packed the car up; I decided today I would drive as she was visibly shaking, and there was no magical cure for this kind of pain. I found a local café, which made us stop and get some food. She insisted she was not hungry, but after some urging, she ate at least part of a pastry. It was not much, but I hoped I could get her to eat more later. I got us a few bottles of water when we stopped so we would not have to stop again on the way.

I pulled up a map to figure out the quickest way. It was about three to four hours away, but I was hopeful I could make it in three. Getting there faster didn't change anything, but I wanted her family to know I did my best to get her home. I had to admit I was concerned about what they would think of their daughter bringing home this older man. But that did not matter; what mattered was getting her home.

I drove as fast as I dared and was sure I was photo-ticketed at least once, if not twice. But again, it did not matter. All I cared about was getting Alessandra home to be with her family. Just before noon, we pulled into the family estate three hours and twelve minutes later. They had texted her saying they would all be there, so that is where we headed. I had barely stopped the car before she jumped out, running to the home, screaming for her mother. Her mother met her just outside the door and embraced her only as a mother could. I decided to stay out by the car and wait to see what, if anything, I could do.

About an hour later, Alessandra walked out; streaks on her face showed she had been crying since she exited the car. As she approached me, she tried to wipe her eyes. I quickly rushed, grabbed her, and told her I was there for her and to please not worry. She told me she had called her friends at the hotel and wanted to know if I still had the address. I assured her I did have the address and could find my way there. "*Okay, why don't you go there? I will come by when I can.*"

"Are you sure? I want to be here for you."

"*I know, but now is not the time. I told my mother you were just a friend I was showing around the country.*"

"I understand, and I will be waiting for you. But know that if you need anything, I don't care what time of day or night you call me. I will come."

She hugged me and said, "*Don't kiss me here, please.*" I hugged her, crawled into the car, and headed towards the hotel.

Once I arrived at the hotel, the owner met me at the door and handed me the keys. I asked how much I owed him, and he insisted it was family, and in times like this, there was no charge. I asked him if there was anything I could do, anything at all. He assured me there was not, but he would let me know if he heard anything. I headed off to the room after parking the car. I unpacked all our bags, mine and hers. I could smell her on every item I unpacked, and it only made me feel her sorrow and pain even more.

I finally fell asleep but kept waking up and checking my phone. I wanted so badly to hear from her, to know she was okay, and to let her know I loved her and would never let her down. Time passed slowly that night. The minutes moved like hours, and the hours felt like days. By the time the sun came up, I was a complete wreck.

I was awakened when I heard a knock on the door. I ran as fast as possible to the door, hoping it was Alessandra. I am sure the owner could see my disappointment when I realized it was him. "Didn't sleep much, did you, last night?"

"No, I didn't. I am worried; what should I do?"

"Listen, put yourself together; we will be holding the wake this evening at the abbey for Alessandra's father. I am sure she would like you to be there."

I agreed, asking where the abbey was and when the wake would begin. He told me it would be late afternoon. Just listen for the bells; I can follow them to the abbey. I closed the door and decided I needed to be prepared. I quickly cleaned up and wore one of my nicer outfits without the cowboy hat. I then sat out for the cafe, realizing I had not eaten since that small pastry I had shared with Alessandra the day before.

When I arrived at the café, the clerk must have seen me coming and met me at the door. She told me to sit, and she would bring me what I had before. I thanked her and sat at the same table Alessandra and I had sat at just days before. Things were so innocent then; we had no idea what fate would bring our direction; now I wish fate had taken a different direction. I could not bear to see her in so much pain. I felt she was being punished for what had happened between us. The Gods were just being cruel, I was convinced.

A few moments later, the clerk brought me my cafe and pastry.

"Have you seen Lexi?"

"No, not since I dropped her off at her grandfather's place yesterday."

"You saw her yesterday?"

"Yes, I saw her, why?"

"*We were all worried. We had not heard from her since that day we saw you both leave here together. Her father had been trying to find her for three days, and we all thought...well, that something bad had happened.*"

"Bad happened..." I stated, "You mean everyone thought I had done something bad to Alessandra?"

"*Yes, I am sorry. We had nothing to go on, and she was not responding to any of our phone calls or text messages.*"

"Oh dear, I am so sorry. I had no idea she had not told anyone where we were." God, how could I have not asked her? Was I so wrapped up in myself that I didn't think about it?

I looked up at the clerk. "I have been with Alessandra since then and had no idea about this. I feel horrible about that. We spent one night at the Winery, three nights in Venice, and another somewhere else."

"*What do you mean you spent one night at the Winery and three in Venice with Lexi?*" She looked at me with a glare. Fuck, I spilled the beans; what was I going to say?

"It was all innocent, I assure you."

"*So where did you stay the night at the winery, the Honeymoon Suite?*"

I could see the simple answer I had given would not cut it. I decided honesty was going to be the best option. With that, I pulled out my journal and gently removed the pages where I wrote about the Winery and Venice. I handed them to her and said, "Here, please read."

"*This is your journal?*"

"Yes, I write in it daily about the prior day and what I did. Please be aware these are my thoughts, and though they might be a bit raw, they should show you how I feel about Alessandra."

She sat quietly, reading the pages one at a time. She seemed to be getting calmer and more comfortable until she turned over and started reading the final page. Fuck, I thought, I wrote about our first night together on that page. Oh, God, now what have I done? At first, she was furious, occasionally glancing up and shooting dagger eyes in my direction. Then something happened. She started crying...

"Are you okay?" I asked her, but I was unsure what response I would get.

"*I can't believe you let Lexi write that in your journal.*"

"What... Did she write something in my journal?"

"*Yeah, you mean you didn't know?*"

"No, I didn't know; she must have done it while I was in the shower that morning when we were leaving Venice."

"*It is in Italian. Can you read it?*"

"No, unfortunately, I cannot."

"*Would you like me to read to you what she wrote?*"

I was speechless and didn't know what to say. Alessandra wanted me to find it, but I was unsure it was suitable for anyone other than her to read it to me.

"*I am sure she has told you already, so I think it is okay for me to tell you.*"

I reluctantly agreed and asked her to read it to me.

> *My silly fool, what have you done with my heart? I had never believed I could ever have found someone who could see me for who I was. I knew fate was playing with us that first day you showed up at my winery. I should have never served you that wine, but something told me I needed to. You have shown me your soul, and though it is scarred from years of pain, all I see is the beauty and compassion you have shown to so many for so many years. You are the most selfless man I have ever met, and you care for others more than yourself. Please allow me to continue to be the one who cares for you for the rest of your days. I am forever your Alessandra.*

As she looked up from the pages and handed them back to me, she could see I was visibly stirred.

"*Are you okay? Can I get you anything?*"

"Yes, I need a pen. I left mine at the hotel and need to record this moment so I will never forget how I feel now."

She ran in quickly and grabbed me a pen. It was not fancy like I had bought myself, but I didn't care. I needed to write what I was feeling as fast as I could as the words were backing up in my heart, and they were necessary. When she returned, I quickly scribbled out every word I felt, the phrase I felt. It was all gibberish, but I knew that someday I would want these words. I thanked her for the pen and everything else. She told me the wake would start around 5 pm and that I should be there. I agreed and asked her for directions.

"*I will come by the hotel, and we can walk together so you are not alone, okay?*"

“That would be very kind,” I responded. She said she would be at the hotel around 4:30 to make sure we had plenty of time to get there. I got up, hugged her, thanked her, and walked off.

Chapter 12

As I wandered through the village, I kept being haunted by the feeling that I somehow was the cause of this tragic event. Maybe I had taken my broken self and unleashed it on Alessandra. The thought was devastating. I kept wandering just aimlessly up one cobblestone road and down another. Where was I going? I honestly did not know. I started to feel like I had so many days prior when I was wandering through the Alps trying to find something, though I did not know what. Just then, an elderly lady stepped out on the path to block me.

"*Sir, are you lost?* This is the fourth time you have walked past my door this morning."

I told her I was a bit lost but would find my way back to the hotel.

"*I did not mean that kind of lost; I mean, you look lost.*"

"I am sorry, I do not understand what you are asking me."

"*Are you lost? You seem like you are wandering our streets and have no purpose.*"

"Oh, I understand now what you mean, and yes, I guess I am a bit lost, to be honest with you."

"*Come inside and have a cafe; maybe you just need someone to talk to help you find your way.*"

I gladly accepted her offer. As I followed her up the path to her door, she pointed to a table with two chairs. "*Have a seat; I will be right back.*" I took a seat and realized I was quite tired. I had no idea how far I had walked, but I was certainly feeling the exhaustion from the morning.

A few moments later, she came out with a tray. She was a bit shaky, so I got up, took the tray from her, and placed it on the table. I then pulled the chair out for her to take a seat.

"*Well, I have not had someone get my chair in a very long time,*" she laughed. As she sat, she began pouring the coffee. She had kindly put a carafe of water with a glass on the tray.

"*Looked like you needed some water; not many people walk as much as you do dressed like that.*"

I had not thought about it, but she was right. I had dressed like I was going to the wake this afternoon, and in the autumn sun's warmth, I was a bit overdressed. I poured the water into the glass, leaned back in the chair, and began to drink it.

"*So, what brings you to my little town?*"

"Honestly, it is a long story, and I don't even know where to begin."

"*Well, the best place to start a story is at the beginning.*"

"Yes, you are right, but I don't know where the beginning is, or was, at this time. I do not even know what story I should tell. It is all so complicated, like stories within stories."

"*Like layers in a cake,*" she said.

"Yes, exactly like layers in a cake, but what layer is the question? I guess I am here because of fate, as foolish as that might sound."

"*Oh, that is not foolish; Fate is a mystery to us all; you never know when it will appear. So how did fate lead you here?*"

So, I started my story, picking up when I got to Italy. She was a very good listener and would occasionally ask me a question or two, but mostly, she just sat opposite me and listened. Just as the story got to the part of Alessandra and me that morning at the cafe, she interrupted me.

"*So, you are the mystery man my Lexi has been traveling with?*"

"Your Lexi? I never used that name for her; I never felt like it spoke to her true self."

"*Yes, she is my Lexi; I am her grandmother on her mother's side of the family.*"

"Oh, okay. Sorry, I had no idea; perhaps I should leave."

"*No, dear, it is nice to meet the man who captured my Lexi's heart.*"

"Captured her heart…" I repeated. Why did I say that out loud? I thought it wasn't brilliant and would undoubtedly lead to a conversation I would not want to have.

"*Yes, but this also explains why you are dressed the way you are; you must be going to her father's wake this afternoon.*"

"Yes, yes, I am. I am going there for Alessandra."

"*Alessandra!*" she laughed. "*Young man, nobody calls her that but her father! Why do you call her that?*"

"I just think it fits her better; it is how I see her in my mind's eye."

"*Well, I am happy someone knows my…Alessandra.*"

"Did you use her full name?"

"*Yes, she is my granddaughter, and she is named Alessandra after her grandmother.*"

"You mean, your name is also Alessandra?"

She laughed and looked at me, "*Yes, I am a Alessandra.*" She phrased it like it was more than a name, which was almost exactly how I felt about it. It was more like a spirit or a Goddess. I must have been mumbling to myself as I was thinking this because Alessandra let out a big laugh. "*So, do you think my Alessandra is a Goddess?*"

Oh shit…I did say it out loud. "Yes, she is a Goddess to me; she saved me."

As I got up to pace, I started to get emotional and wanted to hide my face so Alessandra would not see me. My journal fell out of my lap, and the pages I had removed earlier fell to the ground. I quickly picked them up and hastily put them on the table, not concerning myself with the position. As I walked away, "You speak Italian, I see."

"No, I do not, though I wish I did."

"*Why do you write it in your journal then?*"

I thought, fate, you cruel minx, you have done it to me again. At that moment, she picked up the page that had Alessandra's note to me.

"*Why do you write in Italian if you do not speak it?*" she asked. I turned to face her. By now, she could see I was visibly upset, and a tear streamed down my cheek.

"Alessandra wrote that to me, and until this morning, I did not know it existed."

"*Oh, oh, I understand now. Would you like me to read it to you?*"

I told her, "I had been read it before by the girl at the café who originally found it, but I had forgotten the words while wandering. Would you be so kind? I need to hear her voice."

"Okay, I will read it to you," she responded.

As she read the lovely passage, I fell to my knees. By now, the tears were profusely flowing down my face.

"*Why are you upset?*" she asked.

"I…I guess my heart is breaking because she is now in so much pain, and I feel helpless; there is nothing I can do; all I want to do is take this pain from her, so she does not have to suffer anymore."

"She will be fine, young man; it takes us Italian women time. When you love so much, the pain is to be expected. She loved her father very much; they had a very special bond. She will be in pain for a long time, but she will not give up the pain, as it is a reminder of the memories of him. Do not try and take away her memories of her father. You understand what I am telling you, young man?" That was now the third she had called me a young man.

"Say, Alessandra, why do you always call me young man? You know I am not young anymore. I have many years behind me, like yourself."

"*Yes, this is true, but from my point of view, you are still very young.*" I can see her point; I guess age is relative to your current situation."

Responding to her earlier question, "Yes, I do get your point; you should never trade all the good and precious memories simply to remove the pain from the loss."

"*Good boy, now you are starting to understand. You love my Alessandra, do you not?*"

"Yes, I do, I do very much so." I handed her the other torn pages from my journal and told her she could read for herself. I was so far down this rabbit hole that I knew there was no turning back. Even though it was embarrassing, I knew it had to be this way. She took the pages from me after I put them into order. She then sat quietly and read them carefully. Her hands shook as expected with age, and she struggled to keep the pages still enough to read.

"Alessandra, would you prefer I just read them to you?"

"*Would you mind? My eyesight is not what it once was.*"

As she handed me the pages back, I saw her eyes for the first time. She had always been looking downward towards her feet. "Alessandra, she has your eyes!" I exclaimed.

"*Yes, my boy, she does.*" I stared at her eyes; the similarities were uncanny.

"S*o, you going to read me what you wrote about my Lexi?*"

"Oh yes, of course, I am sorry I was caught up in—"

"*My eyes, yes, I know. My Francisco looked at me much the same way. Thank you; it reminded me of how he saw me so many years ago.*"

With that, I decided to read what I wrote. I decided to go back one page to the afternoon I first met Alessandra. She laughed when I read the comment about first time at the winery. I am sure I turned about ten shades of red and even laughed at myself a bit. I didn't read much to her about my troubles, but enough to give her the context of all the expletives Alessandra had hurled in our torrid race to the winery that day. I told her about the many bottles of wine and the kindness she had shown me after listening to my tale. I then told her we had to stay the night in the Honeymoon Suite at the winery, though I was pretty nervous to bring it up. I mean, what was she going to think?

"So that was you two in the room last week?"

"Uh... I guess it was, but we called it the Non-Honeymoon suite, as Alessandra made it very clear the couch was my bed for the night."

"*Good for her,*" she said with a chuckle and a grin. I continued the story about our many nights in Venice and how we had eventually crossed that barrier into...love, I guess.

"*So, that must have been when she wrote to you that lovely note?*"

"Yes, I guess it was." I thought back to the words she had written, so simple but poignant.

"*Well, I think it is time to get cleaned up for the wake. Please, come again tomorrow and let us chat some more.*"

"Gladly, what else was I going to do?" It was lovely talking to her, and she connected me to Alessandra, whose pain weighed heavy on my heart.

When I returned to the hotel, the café clerk was standing there waiting for me. "*You're late; we have to go.*"

"I am so sorry; I was visiting with Alessandra, and time just away from me."

"*You saw Alessandra, is she okay? How is she? Please, tell me.*"

"Oh, I am sorry; I meant I was with Alessandra's grandmother, whose name is also Alessandra."

"*Oh... We call her Nonna Alexa so that you know in the future.*"

"Noted, and I will make sure to remember that. Hey, speaking of names, what is yours, please?"

"*Oh, I am Rose, and you are?*"

"I am Nathaniel, but my friends call me Nathan."

"*Okay, Nathan, it is.*"

We walked briskly towards the abbey, just talking about next to nothing. When we arrived, the family was seated in the front of the small chapel facing the entry. Rose and I entered and were ushered down the left side of the abbey to a line of people already there ahead of us. I could see Alessandra between her mother on the far right and her grandmother. They were all in black, as expected, but you couldn't see their faces as they all were covered with veils.

I had never really attended a wake, so I did not know what to expect. As the procession moved, we eventually found ourselves next in line. Rose leaned over and told me she would lead and introduce me to each person as Lexi's friend. The first three people were all siblings of Alessandra's. I barely got their names as I kept glancing up the line at her.

I just needed to see her face; I needed to hear her voice. Next in line was her father's father. Rose introduced me, and I expressed my condolences. He reached out his frail but still stern hand. He leaned in and thanked me for coming, but then, as I went to pull my hand away, he pulled me back. "I would like to speak with you tomorrow. Please come to the winery at noon."

I agreed, and he let my hand go free. Next was Nonna Alexa, as they called her. Rose went to introduce me, but Nonna Alexa spoke, "Oh, I know this fine young man; we met earlier today."

At that moment, Alessandra glanced over at me. I could not tell if she was upset with me or just upset in general, but I felt like I had somehow broken trust with her. I was terrified…I extended my condolences, and Nonna Alexa thanked me and reminded me I was to come to visit her the next day.

"Yes, I will come by in the morning before I go to the winery." She nodded her approval, and then I moved to Alessandra.

As I reached for her hand, she snatched it away. "What are you doing here? And what are you doing talking to my grandmother, and what are you going to the winery for?" Her stare was intense, and she was distraught with me.

Nonna Alexa leaned over, "Please, Alessandra, don't be mad at him. I stopped him on the path and asked him in for a café. He was perfectly polite and was a treat to talk to. I do not get many visitors anymore, you know."

With that, Alessandra let up on her bear grip on my hand, and her eyes softened. She burst into tears, and instinctually, I grabbed her and held her as only I could. She leaned into my shoulder as I got down on one knee. I placed my arm on her back like I was trying to defend her from some evil that was attacking her. At that moment, her mother leaned in.

"It will be okay, dear," she whispered to Alessandra. "You should go with this kind man."

Alessandra looked at her mother. She could see she was smiling, even through all the tears. I would later find out that Nonna Alexa had told her mother about our visit and about the words Alessandra had written to me and the words I had written about her. She looked over at me. "Please, take her and be gentle with her. She loved her father very much."

She lifted Alessandra from her chair and into my embrace. Rose was still standing there, so she helped me get Alessandra to her feet. We walked to a small side door leading out from the abbey into a garden. Rose helped me walk her to a bench where I sat next to her, then she looked at me. "You better not break her, cowboy."

I knew exactly what she meant. Hell, I was still a broken man, yes. I was on a path towards a better place but was not there yet. With that, she walked away and back into the abbey. I sat with Alessandra for the longest time. She just leaned into me and cried for what seemed an eternity.

After more than an hour of crying, she started to compose herself. You could tell this was a burden she had been unprepared to carry. Indeed, at least not yet. Her mother and Nonna Alexa entered the garden to check on her. She told me the wake was over, and it was time for them to go. She thanked me for comforting her daughter and hoped I would drop by her home sometime after the funeral. I said I would be honored to visit with her and appreciated the invitation very much. With that, she told Alessandra it was time to go. I got up and helped her to her feet; she leaned in, "Thank you, my fool. I love you so very much. Please be patient with me."

"I love you too, my Alessandra, and I will always be here waiting for you."

She took her by the arm and headed back to the abbey. Nonna Alexa stepped over to me. "*You are a good man; I see a bit of Francisco in you. You take good care of my Lexi.*"

"Did I just get your blessing?" I asked her.

"*Oh no, it is not my blessing you need.*"

"Then whose, whose blessing do I need?"

"*You will figure it out; just be here for her.*"

"Of course, I will; I could not imagine not being here for her."

"*Do not forget, I will see you for café in the morning. Let us say 9:30, okay?*"

"Yes, that sounds perfect; I will see you then."

I stood in the garden for quite a long time. Finally, I saw Rose entering. "Hey, Nathan, do you want to go to eat?"

"Yes, please; I have not had a real meal in several days." She smiled and motioned for me to follow her. As we left the abbey, we started the trek back to the village. We walked quietly, as it was a sad moment for all. She took me to a small restaurant where we quickly ordered a meal and wine. I was very aware of the pain in my heart, so I sipped my wine sparingly, as I knew the slippery slope that would follow. A few minutes into the meal, I asked her, "Hey, Rose, you whispered something in Alessandra's ear the other morning. What was it?"

She about half choked on her food and then started laughing.

"*You mean she did not tell you?*"

"No, she did not; please, would you be kind enough to let me know?"

"*Well, normally I would not, but I see no harm in this situation. I have no idea what the two of you had been talking about, but it must have been...hmmm, how shall I put this? Erotic, yes erotic.*"

"Why would you think that? Our conversation had not been of that nature. Well, except for her and my jacket."

"*Well, according to your uh-hmmm, you know what I mean. Something she said had gotten your attention.*"

Shit, she had noticed, I was right, that was what they had giggled about.

"Yeah, okay, you caught me. She was talking about rolling around in her bed naked in my jacket if you must know."

"Well, that is certainly a vivid picture, which would explain it."

I guess... We both laughed about it and returned to our meals. After a bit, I asked her if she knew why Alessandra's grandfather wanted to see me at the Winery the next day.

"Nope, I have no idea, but I would not want to be in your shoes having to explain the Honeymoon Suite." She laughed loudly. "*Do you have a next of kin I should contact in the event?*"

"The event of what?"

"*You do not understand Italian fathers and their daughters, do you?*"

"No, not really. Is it that different than any other father and daughter relationship? he was her grandfather, I thought..."

"*Well, you will find out tomorrow; I hope to see you the next morning in one piece.*" With that, I slammed what was left of my wine, grabbed another glass, and started on it.

"Shit, what mess has fate gotten me into now?" I spoke.

Rose replied, "Wow, Lexi has had an impact on you."

"What, huh, why would you say that?"

"*She is always going on and on about how fate does this or that. What you just said sounded like something she would have said, is all.*"

"Wow, you are right. I did sound like her." I smiled as I knew even though she was not with me, a piece of her would always be. We wrapped up our meal and went our separate ways; I hugged her and thanked her for being kind to me today. She acknowledged and hugged me back, "See you tomorrow." Then disappeared down the alley. I spent several hours wandering the village square, my mind racing from everything that had happened that day. What would fate bring me tomorrow? It haunted me…

Chapter 13

As the sun peeked into the window in my room, it brought me no peace or comfort. I knew today was going to be tough. But I knew also that it was something that had to be done. I quickly hurried off to the café to get a quick bite. Rose met me at the door with my cafe and pastry. As I sat down to eat, she leaned in, "*You know I was kidding last night about her grandfather and your demise. Right?*"

"No, no, I did not. I am completely freaked out and have no idea what to expect."

"*Relax, Nonna Alexa will explain it better than I will. Just know if he did not want you around, you would have no place in this village to stay. We are all protective of our families.*" Saying that, she spun on her heels and went back to the café. As I sat at the table where Alessandra had teased me many days prior, I swear I could smell her essence. I know I couldn't; that would be impossible, but I could. I finished my meal and returned to the hotel to get my dragon, as I would need it to go to the winery in a few hours. It was a long walk back to the hotel from Nonna Alexa's place.

When I arrived at Nonna Alexa's home, she had already set a tray on the table where we had been the day before. It seemed some pastries and some cafés were waiting for my arrival. She saw or maybe heard my dragon pull up. She stepped out the door and waved as I exited my car and walked towards her.

"*Nice car there, young man. You know my Francisco used to have one that was, well, identical to that one. Now that I am closer, I can see it better.*"

"Are you sure?"

"*Oh yes, he loved his little Dino.*"

"Wow, what are the odds of that?" The production numbers on the Dino were minimal.

"*Do you mind telling me where you bought this lovely car?*"

"Sure, it was in a private collection just outside Modena."

"*Modena, the Museo Modena?*"

"Yes, that is exactly where I got it; why?"

She quickened her pace and kept looking at the car. She walked past me like a guided missile heading to my Dino.

"*Do you have the Logbook?*"

"Of course I do."

"*Show it to me. Show me now, please.*"

"Yes, yes, let me get it." I hurried to the car and retrieved the book. By this time, she had reached the car and caressed it, much like I would caress Alessandra. She took the book from my hand. There was a purpose in what she was doing.

"*Oh Francisco, your car, I have found your beloved car.*"

"Huh, I am sorry, what? I am confused."

She opened the book and turned to the page that recorded the car's ownership. She used it to confirm the providence. A few lines above mine, with her finger, was a name: Francisco Guillermo Ferrari.

"*That is my husband, my beloved Francisco.*"

Sure enough, it was Francisco, but Ferrari was the last name. Indeed, it could not be the Ferrari. I looked at her. "So, your last name is Ferrari?"

"*Yes, yes, it is, but not the same family as this Ferrari,*" as she gently petted the car. I looked at her; her face was beaming with life, not frail as the day before.

"*Let us go sit; we have much to discuss.*"

I would say so; somehow, I have her husband's Ferrari. I thought, well, fate, you have outdone yourself this time, that is for sure. When we reached the table, I poured our café.

"Nonna Alexa, how—"

"*Nonna Alexa, am I now? I see.*"

"Oh, sorry. I was told that is what everyone calls you."

"*It is, but I like it when you call me Alessandra; it reminds me... Just call me Alessandra when we are alone. Okay?*"

"Of course, Alessandra." Starting my question again, "Alessandra, why did Francisco sell his Dino?"

"*Well, my boy, that is a tragic story. When my daughter married Alessandra's father, he wanted to buy back the portion of the winery his father had lost many years before. It was essential to him and his father; our daughter loved him so much. Francisco sold his car to help them raise the money to repurchase it from the owners. But fate had a different plan.*"

She continued, "*When Alessandra was born, there were complications, and she required special care that we could only get in Roma. So, instead of spending the money to buy the property, we had to use that money to help Alessandra. Francisco always said it was the best money he had ever spent, but I knew in his heart he truly missed this car,*" as she pointed to what was now my car.

"Does Alessandra know?"

"*No, we did not want to burden her with this. We had planned on telling when she got older, but my Francisco passed before he had the chance.*"

"When was that, if I may ask?"

"*Oh, several years ago. He was delivering wine to a resort in Brunico, and there was a terrible accident. A truck lost control coming down the mountain, and many people were hurt, and several, including my Francisco, were killed.*"

I sat in horror. Could it be the same accident that had killed my Francesca? I pleaded with her, "Do you remember the date?"

"*It was the last week of August in 1988, I believe; yes, that was when.*" I could not believe it. "*What's wrong, Nathaniel?*"

I looked up at her, "You used my real name?"

"*Yes, yes, I did. Is that okay?*"

"Oh, of course, I had gotten used to the *young man* and *my boy*."

"*So, tell me, what is wrong? You look ill. You are as white as a ghost.*"

"I am sure, It is ironic that you say I look like a ghost. I have something I need to tell you."

So, I started. I told her about Francesca; she remembered her name from my prior conversation with her.

"Do you remember I told you she was killed in a tragic accident?"

"*Yes, yes I do... Was the accident in Brunico?*"

"Yes, it was the last week in August 1988." We both just sat there, really not knowing what to say.

"So, your Francesca and my Francisco were killed in the same accident. Your meeting and falling in love with Francesca led to your journey to my village and meeting my Lexi. And now you are driving my Francisco's Ferrari."

"Yes…yes…yes."

The air was heavy, and there was no way to escape the situation. Was this fate? And if it was, was it fate being cruel or trying to make up for some tragic mistake that had taken her Francisco and my Francesca? Our coffee had gotten cold, and a rain shower was on the horizon.

"Alessandra, may I ask you a favor and a question, please?"

"Sure, Nathaniel."

"Let us not tell anyone about this just yet; I feel this news could be too much for them to digest."

"Yes, I agree, for now. But one day, we will need to tell them together."

"Yes, it would be best coming from both of us."

"So, what is your question? It is about to rain?"

"Oh, whatever became of the property that Alessandra's father and his father were trying to buy?"

"It is still there; it is next to the winery. It used to be one estate that Lexi's great-grandfather owned."

"What happened for them to sell that parcel?"

"You said one question, that is two. You can ask Lorenzo."

"Who is Lorenzo?"

"Lexi's grandfather. It is time for me to go in. You drive safe, the roads will be wet. Come visit again tomorrow, if you please."

"Of course, I will visit. I have so much more I want to know." With that, she picked up the tray and headed into the house. Just as she was about to walk in the door, she waved and smiled at me.

When I got to the winery, the rain had passed. It was about ten minutes out of town, but I missed the turn again, so I was late. I thought to myself, *Great first impression, fool.* There it was. I was now calling myself a fool, just like my Alessandra. I sat there with a stunning expression when a bang knocked on the door window.

"Hey, you going to get out of that car?"

Crap, it was Lorenzo; I had no idea of what I was going to say or do. I was petrified…

"Yes, Sir, I was just putting away some papers into the box."

I took the logbook I had taken out and put it in the box. Once it was secure, I stepped out of the car. Lorenzo was a lean, weathered man with an angular face and a firm chin. "*Let us sit in the garden, Nathaniel, I think it is. Is that not your name, lad?*"

"Yes, Sir, that is my name."

"*Good, I did remember it. I am Lorenzo, and by now, I am sure you know I am Alessandra's grandfather on her father's side of the family.*"

"Yes, Sir, I am aware."

"*Good; now that introductions are over, we need to speak about things.*"

Things…things…I pondered, even fretted over things and what all that could entail. As we walked, I noticed he had a limp in his stride, not like arthritis, but more like an injury.

"Sir, may I ask how you got your limp?"

"*Lorenzo is my name; call me Lorenzo, and as for the limp, it came from an accident.*"

"An accident. Was it the same accident that Francisco was killed in?"

"*So, you're learning our family history, I see, but no, it was not that kind of accident.*"

"Oh, then, may I ask what kind of accident?"

"*When I was a young man, I wanted to race cars. It was my entire life. I worked hard to get on any team I could, but I could not find a sponsor. My father, Alessandra's great-grandfather, offered to support my passion, but it would cost me my inheritance. He said that if I wanted to do this, he would sell half of the estate and give me the money, but the other half would go to my brother. I agreed to his terms; I was not a winemaker as he was, and my brother is now. But after getting on a team, I got in a horrible accident. I shattered my pelvis; it took many surgeries and many months before I was even able to walk. My days of racing were over, and that was that.*"

"I am sorry to hear of your misfortune. I am sure it was painful not just to lose your dream but also your inheritance."

"*Yes, it was, but I got work as a mechanic for a time working on a racing team.*"

As we got to the garden, "*Nathaniel, let us take a seat. I am an old man, and I need to rest.*"

"Of course, we can sit."

We came to the first table and took a seat. "Can I get you something to drink, Lorenzo?"

"*Yes, go get me a nice glass of wine. And you better get one for yourself as well.*" Why did he phrase it like that? You better get one for myself. What did fate have in store for me that afternoon? I quickly went to the winery; nobody was there, so I grabbed a bottle and two nicer wine glasses and returned to the table. I poured Lorenzo his wine and then one for myself. We sat there, sipping the wine, "*So I suppose this is where it all happened.*"

"What happened?" I asked, fearing the answer.

"*Where you met our Alessandra.*"

"Oh, that, yes, this is where it happened."

"*Well, tell me more, why did you end up here at this winery in our little village?*" I decided by this time that so much of the truth was known in the village, and there would be no point in not telling him about it.

"Well, Lorenzo, it is not a simple story."

"Good thing you got us a bottle then, I guess."

"Yes, I guess it is."

He was a very matter-of-fact kind of person. He used words effectively when he spoke. He spoke what he meant. I told him why I had come to Italy, how I had struggled to find a purpose, a reason to live honestly. I told him how I had traveled to Brunico and through the mountains in search of solace. I even told him about my thoughts on top of that ledge. I finally got to how I arrived at the winery so many days ago and how Alessandra had been such a gracious host and served me even though they were closing. I did, however, leave out the part about asking to stay at her place, as I did not want to get shot. I then told him how she got me a room at the village hotel and how I had, *by fate.*

"*I have heard that term; Alessandra has used that term forever.*"

By fate, she came to the same café where I was getting breakfast. I told him how she and I spent the day together, leaving out my scarred past and the expletives. I told him how we had come to the winery and, yes, how we needed to stay the night as we had drunk too much wine. His eyes gazed through me like lasers, trying to cut my head off.

I quickly explained how it was the Non-Honeymoon Suite, which seemed to reduce the intensity of his gaze. I then told him how she had offered to give me a tour of Venice. By then, I realized there was no way to avoid what would transpire. There was no denying I was going to have to confess.

"Lorenzo, do you mind if I go get something from my car?"

"*Certainly, but get another bottle of wine on your way back.*"

Off to the car, I went to get my journal. I had decided it was better just to let him read my words, feelings, and thoughts, as well as those of Alessandra's, instead of trying to massage the conversation into a hollow truth or, worse, a lie. I grabbed my journal, quickly entered the serving room, and picked up another bottle of wine. When I got back to the table, Lorenzo showed me his empty glass and the bottle. I got the hint, opened the bottle, and started pouring the wine.

"*What is that book you have there, Nathaniel?*"

"Well, Lorenzo, this is my journal. I recorded my daily thoughts, and Alessandra also wrote something in there. I would like you to read it if you would indulge me."

"*Sure, give me that thing.*" I took the three pages from the book, but I first handed him the final page with Alessandra's note.

"Listen, Lorenzo, you may not like what you are about to read, but I want you to read it all before you pass judgment. Can you do that for me, for Alessandra?"

"*Yes, I suppose. Just give me it.*"

"Here, read this first, just the Italian part." I handed him the page; his eyes bobbed back and forth as he read the words Alessandra wrote. He got very silent and even a bit choked up.

"*She wrote this to you, you, Nathaniel; I want to know, did she WRITE THIS TO YOU?*" he screamed.

"Yes, Lorenzo. She did; I can't even speak, much less write Italian."

"*Do you know what this says?*"

"Yes, Lorenzo, I do; her grandmother read it yesterday to me."

"*So, what do you say about all of this?*"

"I am sorry, Lorenzo; I am not sure what you are asking me."

"*Do you love her, too? That is what I am asking you. It is a simple question: Are all Americans as much a fool as you?*"

"Lorenzo, please let me read you what I wrote about your Alessandra; I believe it is the best way for me to answer your question with full honesty."

"*Well, get to it, lad.*"

Now I was a lad, I thought. I had been Nathaniel just minutes ago. I knew I needed to be brave and honest and let him understand how important Alessandra had been and now was to me. I took the pages from the journal and began to read.

"*You write funny; this is all gibberish.*"

"Please, bear with me." I continued to read, leaving nothing out, not a single word, phrase, emotion, and not even our night of passion. After I finished, I looked at Lorenzo. He gazed off at what must have been the property his father had sold.

"*Funny how, what is it she says, Fate, yes, that is it. It's funny how fate has led you to our doorstep. You know, my son and I were about to purchase back the property and reunify the winery. But his death has left us, well, he has just left us, and now there is nobody to take up the mantle. I am too old, and my brother's children have all moved to other parts of the world. I guess our little village was not enough for them. There seems to be no purpose in repurchasing it all now, does there, no purpose at all.*"

He continued, "*We have no heirs to leave it to even if we did reunify the properties back into what my father and his fathers had for generations before. You know, this is one of the oldest wineries still owned by the family that founded it. Our blood has toiled these vines since the times of the Romans through wars, droughts, fires, and many deaths. But now it appears it will all come to an end. My brother is dying; he has cancer and has only a few months to live. I had truly wanted to put this all back together for my son, from whom I took so much. My childish fantasy cost not me but my son and his children everything.*"

I could see a tear running down his cheek. "Lorenzo, did your son have other children who would want to keep the winery in the family?"

"*No, I am afraid not; all they see is the money they can make from selling it.*"

Then, out of my mouth, without me even knowing, I said, "I will buy it, and Alessandra and I will run it and keep it in the family." I was horrified at what I had said. What would he think, or even worse, what would Alessandra think…

"*I think we have spoken enough for one day, and it is time I get home.*"

"Okay. Do you need a ride home, Lorenzo?"

"*No, I will be fine; I couldn't ride in that car anyway at my age.*" As he started walking away towards the back of the winery, he turned. "*So, you love our Alessandra. Do you think you deserve her, her love?*"

"Honestly, Lorenzo, I do not know. What I can tell you is I will spend every day for the rest of my life always trying to deserve her love."

"*Hmm, not a bad answer for an American cowboy.*" He laughed as he walked down the path.

"Lorenzo, when can I come to see Alessandra?"

"*After you speak to her mother.*"

Interlude
Shall I Burn My Ship?

Returning to my car, I could not believe what I had suggested. Did I say it? Is this really what I wanted? My heart screamed yes, but if I did this, I would need to liquidate most of my assets. When I left home, I had sold much of my stuff but held onto a few things. Mostly, I held onto my estate; it was so much about who I was. I spent years carving it out of the weeds and the stone. I had many memories of that place—beautiful sunsets and wine-soaked memories with friends. But they were memories, as most had moved with their own life stories to other areas. The hard truth was they liked being around me because I told good stories, as I had been told many times. I am okay with that, but now that I think about it, maybe they left because I had no more stories to tell. At least none they had not heard before.

As I drove back to the village, I found my mind telling my stories to me. One by one, they played like tiny novels in my head. They had been fun to tell then, but now they felt empty and hollow. There were no great tragedies or romantic moments; they were just stories of somewhere I had been or something I had done. Oh, God, they were propaganda; I had used my stories to promote myself. When I reached the hotel, I decided to head to the village square. There was a lovely little café where I could get some food, and certainly, they would have wine. Sophia's "try the wine" now took on a new meaning.

As I walked to the square, I pulled out my phone; I had used it so little since I had arrived in Italy more than a month ago. I had yet to notice all the emails, though probably junk, and the text messages I had received. Arriving at the café, I ordered my meal and a bottle of wine. As I waited at my table for wine, I decided I would at least scroll through the messages to ensure I had not missed anything important. The waitress soon returned with my wine and poured my first glass. It felt odd drinking alone; the last time I had done that was before Alessandra.

I looked at the ruby red wine and saw her lips in my mind. Oh, I miss my Alessandra. I didn't even know how to express what I was feeling. It was something I had never felt before. I decided to call Sophia; certainly, a friendly voice would be good to hear. She had texted me over a week ago to check up on me, and I had not responded. She picked up the phone.

"*Well, I see you're alive; I had wondered if you had drowned in a barrel of wine or something worse when you did not respond.*"

I guess I had called her a few weeks back during one of my sorrow-filled, self-loathing, drunken nights on the road.

"No, I have not drowned, at least not in wine." With that, I paused. I realized I was drowning, but it was not wine, and I stared into the ruby lips of my wine.

"*Nathan, are you there?*" Sophia pressed.

"Yes…yes, I am here, sorry I was having a moment."

"*Okay, dear. Tell me what is going on. Do I need to come to find you?*"

"No, my dear Sophia, I assure you I do not need to be found. I am doing okay, well, honestly better than okay, but it is complicated."

"*Hmm…*"

"Now, Sophia, do not be judgmental. You, of all people, should cut me some slack, please."

"*Okay, I will cut you some slack, as you say. So, tell me how you have been. The last time we spoke, you were, well…drunk…*"

I decided I wanted to tell her about Alessandra, so I told her about my tale from the first night at the winery to my conversation with Lorenzo. With her, I told everything, but maybe not as vividly as she would have told the story to me. Some things should stay between the lovers who created those memories. But I gave her enough details so that she could get a clear picture of Alessandra and how we felt about each other. I read the passage in my journal to her, though I could barely pronounce many words. But she helped me and snickered, "*You know, you need to speak Italian if you are going to live here.*"

"What do you mean to live here?"

"*Well, I assume you are buying a winery, are you not?*"

Oh yeah, when I told my tale to Sophia, I told her about Lorenzo and the winery. "Honestly, Sophia, I am torn."

"*Torn over what?*"

"Well, if I do this and Alessandra rejects me, or worse, gets bored and tired of me, what will become of me? I guess I am scared."

"*Scared of what?*"

"Scared of losing her, I suppose."

"*Let me get this straight: you are scared to buy the winery because you might lose her. Is that what you are telling me?*"

"Yeah, I guess, though, now that you say it back to me, it sounds like I am being a fool."

"*Yes, a fool you are Nathan. Look at what she said; those are not words from a woman who will get bored. Sure, you will get old, we all do, but your garden is barren, and you need to be happy. Please be happy for me, Nathan; you have only thought of others for so many years. You are still a bit broken, but I can see how far you have come. If Alessandra is the cause of this, you need to trust in your heart. All will be for the best.*"

She was right. I was scared and felt like I was jumping out of a plane without a parachute. If she did not jump with me and save me, I would fall to my death, but if I did not jump, I would never know if she would save me. "You know, Sophia, this is like Schrodinger's cat."

She asked me to explain. I explained how Schrodinger put a cat in a box with a radioactive isotope and sealed the box. Now, the cat could be dead or alive, but you will not know unless you open the box. "My life is much the same. I guess I have to open my box and see what happens."

"*Nathan, you are an odd fellow, but you are right. It is time for you to open the box.*" I thanked her for listening to me; it was nice to have a voice with which to discuss things.

I finished my meal and drank Alessandra's lips, which I now refer to as my wine. It was time to make my decision. It was still early enough in the day to call my friend back home. It was time to let go, time for me to jump out of that plane. Scott answered his phone, "*Hey Nathan, what's up, man? You having fun with any of those Italian beauties yet, amigo?*"

"Listen, Scott, I do not have time for this right now. I was hoping you could help me sell what is left of my things, including the estate. I am moving to Italy." There, I said it.

"*Seriously, Nathan, that must be some great fuck to make you do this.*"

"Stop it, Scott! Never talk that way about my Alessandra."

"*Listen, man, I am sorry. I didn't mean to upset you. Who is this, Alessandra? And what has she done to my friend?*"

"Scott, I could not explain it, even if I tried, at least not in a way you would understand. I am not the same person I was before. I have found something inside myself that I had long ago lost. I need to do this. Please sell all my things as quickly as you can. And I mean everything. Even the stuff in my garages; I want it all gone."

"*Wow... You are serious about this. This Alessandra must be an amazing woman. I am happy for you, my friend. I will take care of it and get the funds in your account as quickly as possible.*"

"Thanks, Scott. I will call you next week."

With that, I hung up the phone. Well, I am jumping out of that plane. I drank some more wine and pondered my decision. Though I was full of trepidation, I knew that over the next few days, I would need to trust in fate.

Chapter 14

As the sun peeked through my window, I felt relieved, even inspired. I decided to see Nonna Alexa to tell her about my plan. I wanted to know if she thought I was crazy, but I hoped she would see it more romantically. I hurried off to the café, as I needed some food, and knew I could not show up at Nonna Alexa's house until 9:30 or later. Rose met me at my table; she had learned I was a creature of habit.

"*So, what trouble are you getting into today?*"

Dare I tell her… No, perhaps another time. "Oh, no trouble. I will visit with Nonna Alexa and then attend the burial service at the abbey this afternoon."

"*Can we go together? I hate funerals and…*" asked Rose.

"Of course, we can go together; who else would I go with?" We agreed to meet at the hotel again at 1:30 as the service was scheduled for 2 pm that day.

"*You are a nice guy, cowboy,*" as she hurried back in the door. As always, I sat at the table Alessandra and I had sat at what now seemed an eternity ago. It had only been two days since I had seen her, but the yearning to hold her in my arms, to caress her, and hear her lovely voice with its lilt was beyond comprehension. As I sat there thinking of her, how she made me feel, and the words she wrote, I was resolute with my decision from the previous day.

While asleep, Scott sent me a text saying that an investor had made me an offer on the property. I no longer considered it my estate; that is certainly a sign. It was now just a piece of property, an asset. I texted him back, telling him to send me the papers and that I would find a local lawyer to assist. As I looked at my watch, the one Alessandra made me get in Venice, I could not stop thinking about the wild, even magical chain of events that had led me to this point.

As the seconds ticked away, I realized that time was no longer my companion but the true villain chasing us all. Jumping out of my chair like a horse from a starting gate, I rushed to see Nonna Alexa. I needed her wisdom. It was now a chain of events I had set into motion. Was I being the fool, or was I being brave? I was not sure; maybe a bit of both. When I turned the corner heading to her house, my heart started beating harder with every step. It was like a spring of water was trying to burst out of wall of granite. I had so much to say, so much to do, so, so many questions. As usual, she was waiting for me, standing at the door. "*Where is my Francisco's Dino?*"

"I walked today; I hope that is okay."

"Of course, I just like seeing it. It is like he is here with me; I hope you understand. I think you do now with our intertwined histories."

I laughed, "Yes, we are like grapevines on a trellis."

She nodded in agreement as we both sat in our usual spots. It was an overcast morning; you could feel winter approaching, but it was not so cold as to chase us indoors yet. Just then, Alessandra looked up. "*Oh, look,*" pointing to the sky. It was a beam of sun, cutting through the clouds like a brilliant spotlight from the heavens. No more had I thought it before it cast its bright light on Alessandra and me. The warmth of the rays felt like we were being hugged in a blanket of warmth on that cool autumn day.

"*Thank you, my dear Francisco.*"

I looked at her. "Why are you thanking Francisco?"

"*Oh, for this lovely moment. I felt his warm and gentle hug just now as the sun broke through.*"

"You are joking…I had the same feeling but did not attribute it to anyone as you did. I take it you are Catholic and believe in all that comes with that?"

"*Well, Nathaniel, it is not that simple. Yes, I am Catholic, as are all good Italians. But I am not naïve either. As you grow up, you need the church; it provides a fabric by which we live our lives. But as you grow, you realize the truth is much more complex.*"

"Do you believe in God, Jesus, and The Holy Spirit, Alessandra?"

"*I guess I do, but not as you are thinking, I am sure. Let me try and explain. Yes, I believe there is a grand design that creates this, and probably many wondrous worlds. But I have lived long enough to realize that blind faith is just being blind to our world. I think of it more like our world is a tiny tidal pool at the sea's edge. The tide brings life to it, and then the tide retreats, leaving us to build our world."*

She continued, "The tide flows in and out as it always does, but our entire history is within the cycle of one tide. I believe that when we pass, we return to the great sea and someday end up in another tidal pool. Sometimes, we end up with some of the same souls that we have been with before. And sometimes, tiny ripples in the sea will return us to our former pool. All our stories are related as if we are one and the same. Do you understand what I am telling you?"

"Yes, I do. You believe we move in and out of this life, or as you refer to it, a tidal pool. It's like reincarnation, but not a guaranteed one. It would all depend on the ripples on the sea."

"Yes, Nathaniel, that is what I mean. And when we are out in the vast sea, we can look into the tidal pool and see all those we have left behind. Those that we love and those that loved us. If the love is strong enough, the tears we shed form the ripples on that vast sea, and perhaps those ripples might connect us to them once again. Maybe fate is just the tears of those who loved us."

I must have drifted off in thought; as she said, this was an excellent way to think of the vast sea.

"Alessandra, do you think your love for Francisco may have been part of what brought me to this place?"

"*Yes, I do. He and your Francesca must have a hand; this is the moment. Maybe they are the hands driving yours and my Lexi's fate. Perhaps this was their grand design to help all of us heal from their loss.*"

"Alessandra, I need to speak to you about my meeting with Lorenzo. Is that okay?"

"*Certainly, Nathaniel, how did your meeting with Lorenzo go yesterday?*"

"Honestly, I was amazed to get to know him. He told me so much about himself, the winery, and his deal with his father. I also shared my journal with him and the words Alessandra had written to me. It was very, very much a wonderful day. But he told me about the current state of the winery and his brother. And how all the grandchildren want to sell it for the money."

"*It is all very troubling, very troubling. I fear it would break Alessandra's heart even more if the winery were sold. Even though her father had no direct ownership of it, I knew she was spiritually connected to that place, to her history. It is like a lightning rod from which her entire life is drawn. Yes, it will break her heart. I worry much about this. It is so much why her father and grandfather were trying to reunify the properties. Her father would have taken over its operations, and it could have remained in the family.*"

"I know. I KNOW…I have an idea, and it is killing me to tell someone"

"*Well, tell me what great idea you are shouting about.*"

"Alessandra, you know I am a man of means; even though my heart might have been empty, my pockets are not. What do you think about me buying the winery and the other property, reunifying them, and Alessandra and I could operate them?"

"*Well, Nathaniel, I understand what you are proposing, but I am not sure how that keeps the winery in Alessandra's family. Unless you are hoping to become a part of that family… Is that your intention, young man? Is your intention to take care of my Alessandra until death do you part?*"

"Yes, that is exactly what I mean, if she will have me. I know our age difference could hinder getting her mother's approval."

"*You should know in love, yes in love, your hearts are the same age. This will not matter if you truly love her and she truly loves you. So again, I ask, is this your intention?*"

"Yes… Yes, I am going to do this. But I want it to be my gift to her and the family, not that she would feel obligated."

"*I do not believe my Alessandra would have written what she did if her heart was not already connected with yours. Your issue is with her mother.*"

"Yes, I know. I am to meet with her tomorrow. She asked me to come by the day after the burial, which is today. And speaking of, I probably should leave you as I and you both need to get prepared for the service."

"*Yes, Nathaniel, you will need her approval for this. She is a tough but also passionate woman, much like my Alessandra. There is one other thing: Her mother and I would like you to sit with the family this afternoon. My poor Alessandra is beyond grief at this time. We both feel she wants, I mean, needs you to be there for her. Would you agree to this?*"

"Oh really… Are you sure? I am not part of the family, at least not yet. Are you sure the rest of the family will be okay with that?"

"*Yes, it will be okay. I will leave a chair between my Alessandra and myself. I will see you there.*"

"Yes, Alessandra. I will be there. Now, let me help pick up this stuff before I go."

I quickly picked up the cups and saucers and put them on the tray. After helping Alessandra to her door, I walked back to the hotel to prepare myself. I didn't have anything appropriate to wear. I needed a black outfit. As I got to the hotel, I saw the owner and asked him if he could help.

"Funny thing; a delivery from Alessandra's mother came for you this morning. I believe it is a suit for you to wear today."

Thanking him, I grabbed the suit and went to my room, hoping it would fit. I never really considered where the suit came from until I put my hand in the lapel pocket and found a note.

Dear Nathaniel,

This was one of Alessandra's father's favorite suits. I hope it fits you as nicely as it fit him.

Francesca

I sat on the edge of the bed. Was this another cruel twist of fate? Why had Nonna Alexa not told me her daughter's name was Francesca? She knew my history. I stood up and looked at myself in the mirror. The suit was a good fit—not perfect, but well enough considering.

I stepped outside in front of the hotel, this time a bit early as I was late last time, and I did not want a repeat of that. I could see Rose walking up the path, so I walked to meet her. We spoke a bit along the way to the abbey. She commented on my suit, so I told her it was Alessandra's father, and her mother had sent it to me for me to wear today. I also told her I had been asked to sit with the family. But other than that, we walked in silence. When we reached the cemetery, I walked slowly to the front to the open seat between Alessandra and her grandmother. As I sat, Nonna Alexa leaned in, "*Thank you, Nathaniel.*"

"Of course; no thanks needed." I then turned to look at Alessandra, who had quietly reached over and now held my hand. As our eyes met, I could see she was shocked, terrified, or bewildered. I could not tell, but it was unsettling.

She quickly looked at her mother. "Mama, that is Papa's suit?"

"*Yes, dear, but now it is Nathaniel's. I asked him to wear it today and sit with us. Calm yourself, dear; all is for the best.*" With that, she turned back, looking at me.

"*Alessandra, you know I love you; I hope. I am here for you and your family. Just let me help, please.*" Looking down, she gently nodded and squeezed my hand as a gentle acknowledgment. As the other guests came in, we all sat quietly, waiting for the priest to give the invocation. It was all in Italian with some Latin mixed in, I think. I could not understand the words, but I could understand the emotions.

As the service ended, everyone extended condolences to the family. When all the guests had left, each family member placed a rose on the casket individually. Francesca handed me a rose and motioned for me to put one as well. As I did, Alessandra collapsed to the ground beside me. She was utterly bereft and began wailing at the top of her lungs, only stopping long enough to catch her breath.

As I started to reach down and pick her up, her mother grabbed my hand and motioned me to do nothing. Alessandra continued to sit and cry for many minutes as the entire family stood in silence, facing the casket. Then her mother nudged me and motioned me to help Alessandra get up. I stooped down and put my arm around her waist as she threw her arms over my shoulder. I gently stood up, carrying our weights on my legs and heart. We proceeded to the car that awaited the family. As I assisted Alessandra in the car, her mother motioned me also to get in. I did and sat quietly beside Alessandra and held her as she continued to tremble.

Once we reached the family home, we all got out and walked inside. Alessandra excused herself and wobbled her way to the bathroom. I walked into the kitchen where Nonna Alexa and Francesca were talking and preparing some food.

"You did well today, Nathaniel," Nonna Alexa stated.

"*Yes, Mom, he did. Nathaniel, thank you for the kindness you have shown my precious Alessandra. This has been very rough on her. She was very much her father's daughter. It will take much time to heal from this.*"

"Francesca, if I may?" She nodded her approval. "There is no such thing as healing; it is more acceptance. We never truly want to heal. We want to remember all the wonderful things about a person, the experiences, and the love we shared with them. If you heal, then you risk forgetting. I think we adapt and accept, keeping all the good things and recognizing there will always be an empty spot where the person we loved used to be."

Nonna Alexa walked over and gave me a big hug.

"*Well said, Nathaniel, that is exactly how I feel about my Francisco.*"

I looked up to see her mother, who was shaken as she looked stoically into my eyes. She had the same eyes as Alessandra and Nonna Alexa. Then she smiled, "Yes, Mom, I think you were right. He is a good man, maybe even worthy of our Alessandra." Then, turning on her heel and facing me, "If she will have him, and he will honor and cherish her." Then, turning away. Nonna Alexa could see I was stirred up by what Francesca had said. She motioned me to step out the kitchen door to the patio. I did as she wished.

A few moments later, Alessandra came to the patio. It seemed like it had been an age since I had last seen her. So much had happened since the little knoll in the vineyard. Did she still feel the same as she did that fateful day? She asked me to walk with her; I happily accepted and walked by her side. We walked in silence for what seemed an eternity. Finally, I said, "Alessandra, my dear, I know your heart is broken and shattered into so many pieces it is impossible to count them all. And I know you must feel lost and helpless in your anguish and grief. I know there are no magical words I can say, no noble deed I can do that will make all of this pain disappear. But you must know I would if I could."

"I would carry this burden for you if there was only a way I could. But my love, in the end, all I can say to you is I love you; I will always love you and protect you as best as I can. I know I am a broken man, not young, and unworthy of your affection. But I know that without you, I am lost, like a ship on a vast sea without a compass or stars to steer by. I am yours if you will have me for what I am."

She stopped and turned to face me. "*I know, my fool, and you are right; my heart is broken, and I see no path forward unless you will be on that path with me. I wrote a note for you in your fancy journal. I meant it then, and I mean it now. I will be your Alessandra as long as you walk this world.*"

I broke, falling to the ground; I leaned against her, wrapping my arms around her legs. I was crying like a baby; my heart was bursting, and the tears flowed freely. She put her hand on my head. "*I love you, my silly fool.*" I gathered myself, got up, and kissed her passionately. We walked in silence.

"*You know, you are going to have to talk to my mother, my grandfather, and Nonna Alexa. They must all see you for the fool, I mean, the man you are.*" She smiled. It was the first smile I had seen on her face since that morning. And though it was fleeting, it seemed to have lasted forever in my heart.

We slowly returned to the home and patio, which we had left over an hour prior. As we reached the patio, Francesca and Nonna Alexa stepped out.

"Dear, why don't you go inside and get cleaned up? You need to eat something." She agreed and disappeared, but not before leaning in and giving me a loving kiss.

"Nathaniel, let us sit and talk," said Francesca. I took a seat opposite her. Nonna Alexa sat down next to me, I think, to comfort me. I was beyond nervous; my heart was beating out of my chest. Alessandra had said she wanted to be with me forever, but I had to get her mother's approval. What if she disapproved of me?

Nonna Alexa leaned in and whispered, "Just be honest."

She was correct; I needed to be honest. "Francesca, I have much I need to say, and I am unsure how to do this. I would never do anything to hurt Alessandra or any of her family. But I have to speak from my heart. It demands I pour out all its contents so that you may judge me for who I was and who I am."

"*Tell me, Nathaniel, what does your heart contain? But I will not judge; none of us wants to be judged; I only care for my family and my Alessandra and what is best for her.*"

"Yes…I understand," So where shall I begin… Like Nonna Alexa said days before, the best place is at the start. So, I began my tale but went back a bit further. I wanted her and Nonna Alexa to know the person I was before.

Not that I wanted to be that person again, but there were parts of that person that were part of who I am, and those things that were genuine and spoke to qualities I felt were important. I told them, though vaguely, about my traumatic childhood and, yes, about Francesca. She giggled a bit when I told that part. I told them about my companies and staff, making sure to include how we are close friends, and they thought of me more a family now. I then got to my wandering days through the Alps and how I had lost Francesca in late August 1988 in a deadly accident outside Brunico.

"*Mama…is that the same accident?*"

"Yes, dear, it is. Nathaniel and I had decided not to tell anyone this just yet. But in the spirit of honesty, you should also know that the Ferrari he bought back in Modena is your father's Ferrari."

"*WHAT?*" she screamed. At that moment, Alessandra and her brothers, followed by Lorenzo, streamed out of the kitchen. They must have heard her scream.

Alessandra ran to her mother's side. "Are you okay, mama?"

"*Oh...yes, dear. Here, come sit down, and let us all sit down. Nathaniel was telling us about himself. You might as well tell us all at the same time. Would you not agree, Nathaniel?*"

Oh, dear God, even though Lorenzo and Nonna Alexa knew my story, her mother and brothers did not. I must have stammered with uh-ummm a dozen times before Lorenzo opened his mouth, "Oh, he must be telling you about how he is going to buy the winery and the other property and reunify them."

Nonna Alexa: "*Lorenzo, be quiet!*"

Alessandra then leaned in and looked at me, "Is this true? Is this what you want to do?"

Shit, the cat is out of the box; I guess we will figure out if the cat is dead or alive now. "Yes, Alessandra, I want to do this for you as my wedding present to you and your family."

Francesca then barked, "*Wedding... Wedding... Wait one minute; I have not given my blessing to any of this. Alessandra... Do you know about this?*"

"Yes, mama, I love him. He makes me very happy, and I know I will be happy with him forever. I am sorry, mama. I know all of this is horrible timing, and I am still so distraught over Papa. But I only know what I feel." With that, Alessandra lowered her eyes and cowered a bit, waiting for her mother's judgment.

Of course, leave it up to Nonna Alexa to throw fuel on the fire. "Hey, boys, Nathaniel also owns your grandfather's Ferrari."

Oh, fate, you cruel mistress. Oh well, I am throwing caution to the wind. Here I go. "Listen, all of you, please. Just listen. Listen to my heart, for it must speak. I truly do not care if you like me or not. All I care about is Alessandra. Of course, I want you to like me, but I cannot let the fear of you not liking me deter me from professing my adoration and commitment to the person who mended my heart."

"I know I am not good enough for her; I probably never will be in your eyes. But it is not your eyes that I seek judgment or approval from. The only eyes that matter to me are yours, Alessandra. I know enough of your history to feel its pain; I know enough of its history to understand its passion. I am not asking you to accept my decision, but I am asking you to accept and respect hers. She has professed to all of you how she feels, and I have now done the same. And if she will have me, I will be hers forever." Then, with a giant huff, I sat forcefully down in my chair like I was a CEO in a boardroom with a bunch of whiny investors.

"Well, he can sure give a fine speech," Lorenzo said first.

"*Alessandra, is this what your heart is telling you to do? Do you think your father would approve of this man, your fool, as you refer to him? Is this what you need for your happiness, my beloved daughter?*"

Alessandra looked at me for what seemed an eternity, her eyes looking at me and through me like she was gazing into a crystal ball, trying to foretell our future. Just then, Lorenzo spoke, "Nathaniel, here are the keys to my car. I think you should leave us. Alessandra, walk Nathaniel to the car. Nathaniel, we will see you tomorrow; we will all see you tomorrow, but let us do it at the winery. It has better wine and more of it." He handed me the keys to his car, so I got up and excused myself. I waited for a moment.

"*It is okay, dear, walk him to the car,*" was all Francesca said.

It was a short walk, though it seemed like my feet were in quicksand. I looked at Alessandra. "I am so sorry. I didn't mean for this to happen the way it did. Oh, Jesus, this is such a fucked-up mess. Can I fix it? Please tell me, it can be fixed?"

"*All you need to know is I love you and am your Alessandra. Fate has done this for a reason. We will both have to see where it leads, I guess.*" With that, she kissed me.

"*I will see you tomorrow, my silly fool,*" she flashed me a secret smile. I drove back to the hotel; my head felt like I had stuck it in a blender and pressed the frappe button. And if my head was like that, then my heart was a hundred times worse. Dread filled my heart, mind, and soul. I had a hard time falling asleep that night.

Chapter 15

The following day came, my heart was pounding with hope and fear. My phone buzzed. It was Scott.

"Hey Scott, what's up?"

"*Good news, Nathan, I got it all sold, but there are some personal items that you need to come back and deal with. Could you be back sometime later this week or early next?*"

"Can I call you tomorrow? Good God, man, what time is it there?"

"*A little after midnight. I figured it would be easier to catch you in the morning.*"

"Get some rest, dude. I will call you later today or tomorrow and let you know what I can do."

"*Great, that will be fine.*" I hung up and checked to see if I had any other messages. There was a text. Alessandra! She texted me. Shit, how could I have not heard my phone?

"My sweet fool, please do not worry; all will work out and be for the best. With love, your Alessandra." I texted her back. *Il mio bellissimo angelo alato, your silly fool.* I scurried out the door to get to the café. I wanted to see Nonna Alexa before I headed to the winery. See if she could give me some advice.

I arrived at the café, and as usual, Rose met me at my table with my coffee and pastry. "*Well, you kind of made a spectacle of yourself yesterday.*"

"What do you mean?" Thinking to myself, what other horror did I commit?

"*Oh, I heard about it last night from Lorenzo.*"

"Lorenzo, Alessandra's grandfather?"

"*No, her eldest brother, he is named after his grandfather.*"

"Oh… Do I dare ask how bad it is? How…well, fucked am I?"

"*Cowboy, I hope you can, but honestly, her brothers, all three of them, are not pleased.*"

"I guess I can understand. I cannot believe everything happened yesterday. It was not supposed to be that way. If Lorenzo, her grandfather, had not ratted me out to the family, none of this mess would have happened."

"*You should have known better than to tell an old man. They are liable to say anything at any time. Discretion is not something they are good at.*"

"Yes, you are right. I should never have blurted out what I did at the winery that day, but now I was a victim of this cruel fate."

"*Cowboy, I hope you make this right; I can tell your heart is in the right place. But we Italians are steeped in tradition. It is treacherous ground you are walking on.*"

After leaving the café, I got in my dragon and drove to Nonna Alexa's home. She was standing outside like normal, with a pot of café and pastries.

"*I see you drove my car this morning,*" she chuckled.

"Yes, Alessandra, I drove your car this morning." I walked over to the table and sat down.

"*Well, this is a mess.*"

"Tell me about it."

"*How could you?*"

"How could I what?"

"*How could you have asked our Alessandra yesterday; on the day her father was buried? Do you have no shame, no respect?*"

"Oh no, please, Alessandra. Please let me explain; it was not like that at all. It was not planned; it was a twist of fate."

"*Ah yes, fate. She seems always to have her gaze fixed on you and my Alessandra.*"

"Yes, that she does. Though I wonder to what outcome."

"*So, tell me how fate triggered this calamity,*" I told her about our walk and how, in my desire to shelter her, even protect her from the pain, and without even knowing it was happening, I asked her if she would take me, this broken man. Could she love me, even with all the scars? That without her, I would forever be lost.

"*Hmm. I can see how the day's emotions could have contributed to this. But it would help if you still had waited until you spoke to her mother. Now her brothers are dead set against you. They call you stupid cowboy, you know.*"

"Lovely, another nickname, just what I need. What I need is…"

"*Yes, what is it you need?*"

"I need Alessandra more than anything; I would give up everything; I need my cherished and beloved Alessandra; without her, I have no purpose; she is my shelter in the darkness of the night, as I am hers. There is no path forward for me without her. There you have it. I am broken, not because of my past anymore. I am broken because she is not in my life. Are you satisfied?"

"*I always was, my dear Nathaniel, but it was you who was not satisfied. You are so scared of losing her that you are not willing to fight to make her your own. Her brothers are tough, but they will not go against their mother. You have Lorenzo's and my support. And I think my Francesca is on your side, but you need to open your heart to her. Let her see what my Alessandra sees in you. You do that, and who knows what fate will bring you next, but I think she is still smiling on you and our Alessandra.*"

I loved when she referred to Alessandra as *our* Alessandra. It felt like we were connected; I was part of their family, and all would work out for the best. I decided it was time to face the music.

"Do you need a ride to the winery, Alessandra?"

"*I would love to, but I do not think I could get in that car as I am an old lady. Francesca is on her way to pick me up. You should go.*"

"Okay, I will see you there; hopefully, I will not get lost this time."

"*You better not, considering you're buying it for all of us.*" She laughed as she walked in the door. I hustled to my dragon. Maybe I should call it our dragon now, I thought to myself. Both my Alessandra's seemed as attached to it as I was, maybe even more so.

When I arrived at the winery, I saw Lorenzo sitting in the garden, thankfully not getting lost this time. I brought my journal with me and walked over to greet him. As he saw me coming up, he yelled, "*Go get us some wine, Nathaniel.*"

"Sure, Lorenzo, I will be right there."

I walked into the serving hall via the patio entrance, quickly grabbing two bottles and two glasses with the other hand. I made my way to Lorenzo; after pouring him and myself a glass, I asked, "Lorenzo, why did you announce to everyone yesterday about buying the winery?"

"*Oh, sorry, lad, but sometimes it is just best to get it all over at once rather than do it one little bit at a time. It just seemed like the right thing to do. Looking back, maybe I could have kept my mouth shut for a few more days.*"

"Yeah, you think! Man, I am in a lot of trouble with Francesca, not to mention Alessandra's three brothers, who now call me Stupid cowboy!"

"*Yeah, they certainly had plenty to say about you after you left. They are harmless, and like all good boys, if you win over their mother, they will fall in line.*"

"Yes, I know. Nonna Alexa has told me the same thing."

"*Well then, it is decided you must win over Francesca. So, what's your plan, lad?*"

"Plan… Plan, seriously, you think I have a plan? None of this has gone according to plan. I am just a player, and fate is running its course on this grand stage that she has set for me. I guess I will live in the moment and see what happens. But I know one thing: I am not leaving this property without Alessandra in my arms."

"*That's the spirit, lad. Fight for what you know is right. You are right!*"

"Lorenzo, here, hold my journal. I need to go get a few things."

A few minutes later, I returned in full cowboy trail gear, including a long custom-made trail duster that almost touched the ground as I walked, my lasso and a custom-made stag horn knife Sophia had given me as a present.

I put on my best cowboy boots, which I had thankfully left in the car's boot with my duster, lasso, and knife. I clipped a pair of Texas-sized spurs on my boots and strutted back to the patio. When Lorenzo first saw me. I think he thought I had a six-shooter under my outfit. He looked frightened at the sight of me. I was no longer Nathaniel; I was cowboy. I looked at him. "Don't worry. I would never hurt anyone, but they do not need to know that. Just play along with the show."

If I was going to be a victim of fate today, by God, I was going to my grave with my boots on and my hat on my head. I paced feverishly back and forth, waiting for the bandits to arrive. When they walked into the garden, I stood in the center, legs squarely set under my hips, with a crazy look in my eyes.

Before they could speak, "Francesca, please speak with me privately?"

Before she could speak, her eldest son Lorenzo Jr. stepped up. "*You will speak to all of us, or you will speak to none.*"

Great, that is what I was counting on. From years of raising horses, specifically stallions, I knew it was not the size of the dog in the fight but the amount of fight in the dog. I looked squarely at him, taking three slow and deliberate steps forward. As I reached my final step, I used my boots and kicked a pile of dirt onto his nice Italian loafers. "Oh, sorry there, I guess the stupid cowboy does not know his manners."

You could see his face flush. Now, mind you, Lorenzo Jr. was a strapping lad some several years younger than me and about one head taller. He had broad shoulders… "*You better watch your manners around my family, stupid cowboy.*"

At that moment, Alessandra screamed, "Stop this! Stop, please."

I looked at her. "Do not worry, dear; I have hogtied and castrated bulls three times his size. His false bravado does not worry me. You see, I have a magic power."

Alessandra looked at me. "*What magic power, he is going to kick your ass; he used to be a boxer!*"

"Oh, so he has already had his head scrambled. That will make it easier for me to castrate this cow, plus he has nothing to fight for."

Then Lorenzo Jr. took a half-hearted jab, hitting me in the jaw. It certainly hurt, but I was not going to flinch. I told myself I would not back down to this cow. "You know what, Lorenzo, if you want to do this, that is fine by me, but let us get something very clear: I will not leave here today without Alessandra. You may be the man of your family, but you are afraid of dying. On the other hand, I am not; I never have been. I only fear not being with my Alessandra; YOU BIG FAT COW! So, as we say back in Texas," with my best southern drawl: "Let us get this party started!"

With that, I pulled the lasso out with my right hand from inside my duster, and then with my left hand, I reached across and unsheathed the stag-handle blade I had in a cross-chest harness. I then walked over to Lorenzo's table, slowing, making sure my spurs clanged louder with every step. I then raised the blade and drove it deep into the wood table. With that, I spun around, flipped my duster back, and yelled, "Well, come on, COW, let me remove those family jewels!"

I slapped the lasso to my coat, making a loud pop. There was one thing I knew: the bull or stallion has to be afraid of the persona because you will not win on muscle. You must win the fight before you begin the fight. At that moment, I could see Alessandra coming towards me; I could see the pride beaming from her face as she stood at my side with her shoulders back. She looked like a lioness ready to devour its prey. Then, out of nowhere, Lorenzo spoke up, "*Well, lads, I think he is pretty serious. Are you sure you want to tangle with...Cowboy?*"

There was no stupid, he called me cowboy. I looked over and tipped my hat to him for the kind gesture. "Now let's do this, or I will speak to Francesca alone. What is it going to be, you fat cow?"

I yanked the knife out of the table. I gave my best YEE-HAW as the knife came out of the wood, "Let's dance!"—running towards him full gallop.

"*STOP, STOP this now! Lorenzo, sit down...Nathaniel, or should I call you cowboy, I will speak with you privately,*" yelled Francesca.

I walked back to Lorenzo, took off my coat, placed the knife gently on the table, and the lasso over the arm of the chair. He looked up at me and gave me a wink. I took off my spurs, picked up my journal, and headed to the serving hall.

I whispered to Alessandra, "Thank God I did not have to fight him. Love you, my angel."

She laughed and said, "*Go, talk to my mama, you fool, my fool.*"

It always melted my heart when she called me her fool. I did not care that she called me a fool; it just did not matter. I was happy to be her fool.

Francesca had already sat at a table when I arrived inside the serving hall.

"*Get us some wine, please.*"

"Gladly," and again hurried off to the bar, getting a bottle and two glasses. By now, I knew the back of the bar as well as anyone could. I returned to the table; she held my journal, which I had placed on the table when I went to get the wine.

As I poured the wine, "*Well, that was quite a show you put on out there. Are you proud of yourself?*"

"No, I am not, but when it comes to Alessandra, death is a better outcome than living without her in my life."

"*You seem pretty certain of your feelings.*"

"Yes... Yes, I am."

"*Do you think she feels the same?*"

"I do; she has said this much to me."

She sat for a moment and sipped her wine.

"Francesca, I brought that journal here for a purpose. You want to know what my heart feels for your daughter, do you not?"

"*Yes... Yes, of course I do. I do not want her to be some toy you play with and dispose of when you grow tired of her.*"

"I understand; that journal is my raw emotions. It is not all pleasant to read, but if you want to know my intentions, I feel I must let you read it all."

"*So, you are offering to let me read your private thoughts.*"

"Yes, I am, but there are also some private thoughts from Alessandra there. And I want to apologize in advance. I have been with Alessandra; it was not planned. It was not some conquest that I was trying to achieve. It was the aftereffect of falling in love."

"*I see...*"

She sat back in her chair, sipping her wine and reading what I had written and the passage by my Alessandra. She read, drank, and turned each page with slow precision. It was agonizing, but I had to see this through. The way out of this would be the way into whatever fate cast our direction.

When she finished her last glass of wine, she pulled the one page out with Alessandra's words. "*Do you know what she said?*"

"Yes, your mother read it to me."

"*Will you always fight for her like you did today?*"

"Yes, I will protect her as long as she will let me."

"*Okay, well, you stay here. I will talk to Alessandra and her brothers, who I think you successfully scared to death today.*"

She half chuckled as she walked out.

"Francesca... Can I ask a favor, please?"

"*Yes, but only one, so make sure it is good.*"

"Oh, I was not putting that kind of importance on this. Can I have some more wine?"

She roared, "*Cowboy...yes, you can have some more wine.*"

Once she left, I went and got another bottle of wine. Sheesh, I needed a drink. I was spent; I had given all I had; if this did not work, I would be devastated. I could not imagine returning to my former life, and I certainly could not imagine moving forward without my Alessandra. My mind reeled as I sat and drank my wine, playing cruel tricks on me. About that time, Alessandra came in and sat down next to me. "*You going to pour me a glass?*"

"Oh gosh, let me get you a glass; give me a second."

"*That will not be necessary.*" Then, with a grin, she picked up my glass and drank. "*What is mine is yours, and what's yours is mine from now on.*"

"WHAT? Oh, God, does that mean what I think it means?"

"*Yes, my silly fool, I am yours, and you are mine to whatever fate brings our way.*"

I hugged and kissed her now wine-soaked lips. It was my first joy in days, though it felt like a lifetime.

"I need to go thank your mother, brothers, and grandparents."

"*Oh, they have already left; we should correct a mistake we made several nights ago.*"

"A mistake? What mistake?"

"*Oh, you know the Non-Honeymoon Suite?*"

I smiled. "Yes…we should. But first, let's have some wine and celebrate our love for each other."

She agreed, and we returned to the garden to watch the sunset and drink wine. It was a magical night as the stars looked down.

Chapter 16

It was a glorious morning, even better than the ones before with Alessandra. The air was serene, a certainty that our fates would be forever together. As she lay sleeping next to me, I just sat watching her gently breathe. It was so calming; I had found something I had never expected in her. An inner peace that I knew would last me for all time. Just then, she rolled over; her eyes met mine; there was no need for words. We knew what each other was thinking and feeling. It was the quietest moment imaginable, but yet there was so much said. I kissed her and said, "Good morning, my angel."

She smiled. "*Good morning, my silly fool.*"

I laughed. "Can I please get a new pet name?"

"Oh, you want me to call you psycho cowboy instead?"

"No, no, please, no!"

"*You will always be my silly fool.*"

I smiled and agreed it was fitting; I had undoubtedly been a fool more than once with her, and yes, silly.

"*Let us get some breakfast; I am quite hungry after last night.*" She winked and giggled, hopped out of bed, and ran to the bath. I just sat there, stunned and amazed at what was happening. As soon as she was done, I quickly cleaned up myself, and we hopped in our dragon, letting her drive, and headed off to the café. "*Hey, Nathan, why did Nonna Alexa say this was my grandfather's car? Did he have one like it at one time?*"

"Oh boy, that is a long story, so after we eat, let us go see your Nonna Alexa. Does that sound okay?"

"*Sure, that is great. I am feeling much better today and want to see her anyway.*"

When we arrived at the café, Rose rushed out the door and hugged Alessandra. They spoke for several minutes, in Italian, of course, so I could not understand a word. But there were plenty of hugs, laughing, and giggling while looking in my general direction as I took my usual seat.

"Guess you better learn Italian if you want to know what we are saying about you," Rose laughingly stated.

"*She is just teasing you, my silly fool. Rose, stop it.*"

As she giggled, they clearly had and were still talking about me. But I was okay with it. I used to hate being teased or embarrassed; that had all changed. I now took it as something sweet and even endearing. Eventually, they stopped their giggle fest, and Alessandra sat down. She leaned over and kissed me, almost like it was an apology for something. I honestly was in heaven. Alessandra could say anything she wanted, and I would have found something to relish and warm myself with. Soon, Rose came out with our food and cafe; as she put it down, she started giggling all over again.

"*I guess it can no longer be called the Non-Honeymoon Suite, cowboy. YeeHaw, cowboy!*"

Alessandra turned red as a rose in full bloom. "Rose…shut up."

"*Sorry… Nope, I am not.*"

Then she let out one last *YeeHaw* as she walked in the door. Alessandra looked at me and mouthed, "I am sorry."

I laughed like I hadn't laughed in ages. I could not stop myself. I just kept laughing. Then Alessandra started laughing and told me to stop laughing. I do not know how long it went on, but the whole café and everyone on the street looked at us like we were crazy. I tried but as I stopped, I looked at her face and saw she was embarrassed and started howling to the heavens again. I had never seen her so red. It was delightful. Eventually, I got it under control and could stop laughing, but every time I thought back to the moment, I would start laughing again. It was clear that whatever Alessandra had told Rose, she did not want me to know, but not in a bad way. And now that I think back on last night, I remember a moment when Alessandra let out a couple of YeeHaw screams in a moment of passion. I looked at her. "Did you tell her about yelling YeeHaw when you were…?"

"*Shut up, you silly fool, not in public.*" I needed to know nothing more. She had shared some details of our prior night's escapades in the Non-Honeymoon

Suite. I decided to let it drop, but I would certainly remember this for future teasing.

After we had stopped laughing, we finally finished our meal. We then hopped in our car and drove over to her Nonna Alexa's home. She was outside, as I had grown accustomed to seeing, even though we were quite a bit later than my normal morning time. She saw us pull up.

"*Well, I see you lovebirds have survived the night. And from the flushed look on both our faces, it must have been good.*"

"Nonna, stop it. We have just been laughing."

"*Oh, okay, what have you been laughing so bad about that you're flushed?*" I could not stop myself. "Oh, she is embarrassed that she screamed YeeHaw while we were making love last night in the Non-Honeymoon Suite."

Alessandra turned to me, "I am going to kill you!"—but I could see she was trying hard not to laugh herself.

Then, out of nowhere, Nonna Alexa starts howling with laughter.

"*Oh, Nathaniel, you should not have said that she is going to kill you later, you know. Oh, but that is perfect. My Lexi and her cowboy riding into the sunset.*"

We all started laughing, though I had to admit I was laughing the hardest. I had finally got something on Alessandra where I was not the fool. We laughed for a few more minutes and then joined her at the table in her front yard.

Finally, we were all calm, though I occasionally let out a YeeHaw to tease Alessandra. Then I decided it was time to get Alessandra her answer.

"Nonna Alexa, Alessandra would like to know the car's story, and you and I agreed we would share it with her. Do you remember?"

"*Yes, I remember; I think you should tell her as you now own her grandfather's Ferrari.*"

"Are you sure?"

"*Yes. It will be fine.*"

With her approval, I proceeded to tell Alessandra about how her grandfather had sold the car and how that money had been used to pay medical bills from her birth and the complications following it. How her grandfather and my Francesca had both been killed in the same tragic accident and lastly, how I had purchased the car and somehow ended up here with her and her family.

After a moment, Alessandra responded, "*Wow... Fate has been playing in our lives like a starry map in the sky that we have been placed upon until our paths collide.*"

"Whoa, yes, that is a great way to think about it. Fate has brought us together. There are too many strings that tie our lives together. There is no other way to explain it."

At that moment my phone rang, it was Scott.

"Ladies, I need to take this; please excuse me for one moment. Hey, Scott, what's up?"

"*You were supposed to call me yesterday. I need to know when you are going to be here. I have to get all of this stuff scheduled; you know.*"

I could tell he was a bit upset with me. "Scott, I know. I am sorry, and I will explain later. God, you must have gotten up early to call me this time of the day."

"*Yes, it is bloody 3:30 am here. Now, give me a date, please.*"

"Okay, hold on one moment."

"*Hurry up, I want to go back to bed.*"

"Alessandra, by chance, do you have a passport?"

"Yes, why do you ask?" Alessandra replied

"I will explain in a moment. Scott, listen, we will be there in five or six days. Will that work?"

"*Yes, but you better damn well be here, mate.*"

"We will be there, I promise."

"*We, what is this we crap about?*"

"Scott, it is a long story. I promise to tell you when I get there. I will send you my exact travel itinerary as soon as I book our flights."

"*I knew it, you're shacked up with some Italian hottie. I knew it; that is why you are acting this way.*"

"Scott, stop it. Alessandra is not some Italian hottie, and I would appreciate you treating her with the respect she deserves!"

"*Whoa, sorry, man, I was just trying to be funny. Please send me your travel plans. Elise and I look forward to meeting Alessandra.*"

"Thank you, Scott; I will send it all later today. Ciao."

As soon as I hung up the phone, I turned around to see Alessandra standing directly behind me.

"So, I am some Italian hottie to your friend. Is that what you have been telling him?"

"Oh God no, never. Dear, let me explain. Scott did not even know you existed until two minutes ago."

"*Oh, so you have not told your friends about me. Hmmm, I would have thought you would have told them about your love for me. Maybe you do not love me as I love you.*"

"Oh, mother of God, that is not it at all. Listen, Alessandra, I have no close friends, nobody other than you to whom I tell everything. I have no one that I trust, that is all. These are people that I am friendly with, but we are not friends, at least not to that level. Do you understand?"

"*I guess, will I get to meet these semi-friends? Well, if I decided to go with you, I should say.*"

"Please, Alessandra, I beg you, I need you to come with me. I am afraid to go by myself."

"Then why are you going?"

"Well, my sweet angel, I am selling everything, and I mean everything. When I leave this time, other than the people I know there, I will have nothing left of me back there. My life is with you, and I do not want any strings that might try and pull me back. I only want to be here with you. Does that make any sense to you?"

"*So, you will give up everything just for me?*"

"Of course, I am. It is meaningless to me; you are the only thing that matters."

She quickly hugged me and kissed me. "*I am sorry, my silly cowboy, I can be a bit jealous, you should know.*"

"It is okay now. Are you going with me?"

"*Of course, my silly fool.*"

"Great, I need to make our travel plans."

"*Okay, let us head to my mother's home; she still wants to talk to you a bit more.*"

"Nonna Alexa, thank you for your kindness, but we must run."

"Yes, come by anytime. You two have fun, oh and Lexi…" replied Nonna.

"*Yes, Nonna?*"

"YeeHaw!"

Alessandra slapped me on the shoulder, "*See what you have done. Now everyone will know.*"

"Right, like Rose was going to keep it a secret."

"*Well. Fine, let's get going.*"

I grabbed her by the waist and spun her around. "You can YeeHaw with me anytime, my angel."

Then, I kissed her passionately to show her my love. After our embrace, she smiled and said, "Let us go, now."

When we arrived at her mother's home, her brothers came out to greet us. I was expecting another confrontation, but that is not what happened. Lorenzo—I nicknamed him LJ for Lorenzo Jr., though I still do not think he likes it—was the first to step up. He gave his sister a big hug. "It is so good to see your smile, Lexi."

"*Thanks, Lorenzo, but you need to thank the cowboy,*" she said, letting out a soft YeeHaw and winking at me with a smile.

Lorenzo then stepped towards me, and I extended my hand to shake his.

"Hey now, you are not going to get that knife and castrate me, I hope."

He grabbed me and gave me a bear hug. "Welcome to the family, cowboy," he said, taking my hat off and putting it on. I bet I look good in this; maybe I should keep it." I was a bit shocked when the other two brothers came in, patted me on the back, and escorted us into the home.

"Look, mama, the cowboy gave me his hat. Guess he feels bad about trying to castrate me yesterday." He turned and smiled and tipped the hat.

"Yes, that is it, Lorenzo; I felt bad, LOL. But yes, the hat is all yours now. You have earned it!"

"Thanks, cowboy."

Alessandra was so pleased to see her brothers joking around with me. She and her mother just watched as the four of us joked about the prior day's rodeo, as they called it. It felt good to be accepted into the family.

Francesca spoke up, "*Okay, boys, let me and the cowboy have a few minutes. Nathaniel, will you sit with me in the garden for a few moments.*"

"Yes, of course," as I tried to straighten my hair.

I followed her outside, and we sat at the table near a small fishpond. It was full of lily pads but being autumn, nothing was blooming. But I could imagine how lovely it must look in the spring and summer.

"I bet this garden is beautiful in spring."

"*Yes, my Lorenzo built it for me many years ago. It was a very special place for us.*"

"That sounds lovely. The beauty in this garden tells me how much he loved you."

"*Yes, he did love me very much, as I loved him.*" She sat for a moment quietly. "*Nathaniel, I want you to know why I made my decision.*" She then handed my journal back. I had forgotten that she had taken it with her outside when she left me in the serving room.

"I wrote something for you in your journal; I hope you do not mind."

"Thank you. It is an honor, and I am humbled that you would want to contribute to my story."

"*Well, I am contributing more to your story, as you put it, than just a few words. I am entrusting you with Lorenzo's and my most precious flower, our Alessandra. You know, I think Lorenzo would have liked you if only... You know, he had a flair for the dramatic himself. I think he would have loved what you did yesterday. However, at times, I wondered if you would castrate one of my boys,*" she smiled and laughed, "*you showed me not only your heart by letting me read your journal, but you also showed me your fight and your absolute devotion to our Alessandra.*"

She reached and grabbed my hand. "*You know, when I say our, it is not just Lorenzo and myself I am talking about; for now, you are part of that as well. I can tell she is devoted to you as you are to her. There will be tough days, as there are with all great loves, but with this devotion, I know you will both continue to find refuge within the passion of your love and devotion.*"

With that, she took her other hand and grasped my hand. I could feel her trembling. I had been looking down and started to tear up when she said I was part of ours. As I looked up, I could see her tears—reserved but flowing, as were mine. She pulled me over to her and gave me a motherly hug. "You go now; you love our Alessandra. I want the two of you to write a wonderful story on this canvas of your love."

Then she let me go and pointed me to go back to the house. I could hear her weeping as I walked away.

"Francesca, are you okay?"

"*Yes, cowboy, these are tears of happiness for you and Alessandra.*"

I returned to the house and made my way to Alessandra, sitting in the library. She could see I was upset as tears flowed down my face.

I ran to her, knelt, and placed my head in her lap. "*What is it, my dear?*"

"Oh, these are tears of happiness, my angel. Do not worry; I just—"

"*Be still, my sweet cowboy.*"

She put her hand on my head and ran her fingers through my hair, calming me and expressing her love at the same time. In a few moments, I got up and sat next to her. "*Mama, what did she want to talk to you about?*"

"I will tell you one day, dear, but for now, it is something special between us. I hope you understand."

"*Yes, I understand, but I hope you will share it with me one day.*"

"Of course I will. She gave me my journal back, and she wrote something inside it. Perhaps we should read it together."

"*Let us wait. There is no rush. We will know when the time is right to read her words. All that matters is that I love you, and you love me, and my family loves us both, and that love is good enough for me.*"

We spent the rest of the day making our plans. I had to get to the bank in the village and set up an account to wire money to. We had to take care of our travel plans, and I had to meet with Lorenzo Senior and the attorney to start all the paperwork for the winery's reunification. The attorney told me it would take about a week or two to get everything in order.

Lorenzo was beaming; years had been erased from his face. In the previous days, he looked like a tired older man with one foot in the grave, but now he was almost giddy. He called his brother in the hospital to share the news. His brother wanted to speak to me, so I happily agreed to visit him at the hospital in Rome the day before we flew to America. Fly *out* to America. A few weeks ago, I would have said fly *back* to America. This is now my home; what a strange twist my life has taken. That starry map in the sky has guided me to my new home and life.

Chapter 17

After several days of running around, dealing with paperwork, and meeting other friends of Alessandra's, it was time for us to head to Rome to catch our plane. We had to run to the hospital for me to see Lorenzo's brother, as I had promised to come to speak to him before I left. I understood he did not have much longer, maybe only a month or two at best. Alessandra also wanted to see him before we left, just in case he passed before she could see him again.

I got the feeling they were close; she had worked for years with him at the winery. She was the only child in the family who seemed to have any passion for the grapes, as Lorenzo liked to say. We got up early and hopped in her car. She insisted we did not want to drive our Dino to Rome and leave it at the airport. Plus, she had an excellent little Alfa Romeo that was comfortable riding in and could carry more luggage. I let Alessandra drive as she loved to drive, and I had no idea how to navigate once we got to Rome or, as she kept telling me, "It is Roma, you silly cowboy."

I had gotten an upgrade from fool to cowboy after the rodeo at the winery the other day, and I was delighted with that. Though in private, she still called me a silly fool, which became her special name for me that she only said when we were alone. She talked the entire way; she had never been to America and wanted to see and do many things. I could tell she had never traveled to a place that was so vast. She would ask me how long it would take us to get from Texas to the desert or Yellowstone. I would remind her it takes days to get from place to place. That concept just baffled her. "*Well, how long does it take to drive from your home to...say, Florida?*"

"Days, my dear, it takes at least two days."

"*Why does it take so long; do you have to drive slow?*"

"No, we drive pretty fast, well over 120 km per hour."

"*What? 120, and it still takes days?*"

"Yep, America is a big place."

She kept on like this for hours. Our flight was in the evening, so we could see Lorenzo's brother before. When we got to the hotel in Roma, we got a bite to eat and drifted off to sleep. We were both tired from the long drive.

The next morning, we got out of bed and rushed to the hospital to see Lorenzo's brother, Alfonso. When we got to his room, Alessandra asked me to wait outside for a moment, which I happily agreed to. She went in, and I could hear them talking, of course, in Italian. But I could tell it was an emotional conversation. Several minutes later, she stepped out. "*Alfonso would like to speak to you alone.*"

What is it about Italians? Either the entire family or alone, there seems to be no middle ground, I thought to myself. I grabbed and squeezed her hand, kissed her on the forehead, and whispered to her, "I love you, my angel." And then I walked into the room. I could quickly see the family resemblance between Lorenzo and Alfonso.

Alfonso was named after his father as he was the eldest son in the family and was a few years older than Lorenzo. You could see the cancer was taking a toll on him; it was horrible to see as I had been told many stories by Alessandra about her and Alfonso in the vineyards when she was just a young lass. In my mind, he was vibrant and cheerful, and he always singing. Now, to see him here like this was heartbreaking. He asked me to sit by the bed as his voice was frail. "*So, you are the cowboy, I take it.*"

"Yes, Sir, I guess I am."

"*Then where is your cowboy hat?*"

I laughed. "Well, that is a long story, but Lorenzo, Alessandra's brother, is now the owner of my cowboy hat."

"*I see. Did he steal it from you?*"

"No, Sir, I gave it to him as a gift."

"*I thought cowboys never gave up their hats or their boots.*"

"Well, to be honest, Sir, I think my cowboy days are becoming more of my history than my future."

"I see… So, Alessandra tells me you are going to help my brother put our father's, and his father's, before him, winery back together. Is this true, young man?"

"Yes, it is, with your permission, of course. I will do none of this without everyone wanting it to be that way."

"*Well, my boy, my sons will not be pleased; they were looking forward to being playboys and living the fancy life, it seems, but if you are doing this for Alessandra and our families, then that is what it should be. I will tell my boys I have made my decision. Have your attorney send me the paperwork to sign before God taketh me from this place.*"

"Yes, Sir, I will call him immediately. I will help Alessandra and your families."

"*No, cowboy, our families, you are now part of us. Your blood will mix with ours, and you will be known as the cowboy who saved our vines for generations to come.*"

I just sat silently; I had never considered it in those terms. It was a heavy burden but one I was happy to bear.

"*Now go, my cowboy, and please send your beloved Alessandra back in.*" With that, he gave me his hand. I could see it had a family ring on it. I shook his hand and thanked him for his time. As I walked out the door, I said, "*Glad you found Francisco's Ferrari. It meant the world to him. It seems you were destined to heal many of the wounds of our history.*"

I turned, "As your family healed many of my wounds, maybe this was fate's destiny for us."

"*Perhaps you are right…cowboy. Bring me back a hat, will you?*"

"I would be honored, Alfonso."

I left the room and told Alessandra he wanted to see her again. After a while, Alessandra walked out of the room and grasped my hand. "We need to go," she spoke softly. I could see she was visibly upset, but I knew now was the time to just be here, to be beside her, just holding her hand.

When we arrived at the airport a short time later, Alessandra felt better but still sad. She knew there was a chance that would be the last time she would speak to Alfonso. It made me sad as I felt I was taking her away from her family at a time when they might need her, but the family agreed this was the right thing to do.

As Francesca told me, "*My Alessandra needs to heal from losing her father; take her and show her patience and love, help her heal this great pain in her heart.*"

When we got on the plane, we were escorted to the upper deck of the 747.

"*Where are we going?*"

"Oh, we are flying upper class; we will need to sleep so we are not completely worthless when we arrive."

"*I cannot sleep sitting in a chair very well.*"

"Well, we have beds to sleep in."

"*Beds, are you kidding me?*"

"No, dear, we have beds."

"Are they private?" She giggled, flashing that mischievous smile I remembered from the knoll at the vineyard.

"No, not private enough for that, but let us get to our seats and get a drink."

I had been fortunate enough to get us a direct flight from Roma to Dallas. From there, we would rent a car to drive to the Hill Country. Once we got seated, we got a drink and settled in. There were only two other people in the upper class, so they sat in the front, and we moved to the back so it would be easier for us all to enjoy the flight.

As the flight took off, Alessandra squeezed my hand. "*I have never flown before; I am a bit scared.*"

"It will be fine; we all feel that way the first time we do it."

"*Oh, kind of like losing your virginity, I guess. Scared, but once you get over that, it is fun,*" she laughed.

She had such a clever mind. She loved twisting words and phrases to try to make me laugh, and almost always, they did.

"Yes, exactly, and sometimes it bounces up and down hard."

"*Oh, that sounds like fun!*"

She let out a cackle and covered her mouth to try and stop laughing. We joked and kidded each other for quite a while. Then I told her, "Hey, look out your window before it gets dark."

"*Oh my, we are in the air. I had not realized we had gotten off the ground yet.*"

She sat there and stared for the longest time. "*I have been in tall buildings, but this is so, so much higher. You can see just so much, and everything is so small.*"

"Yes, you can. I fly so much and take the grandeur of seeing the world from such a high place for granted."

"*This is how the angels, how fate must see us, you think?*"

"Yeah, maybe we would appear so small to them."

"*Well, she sure found us out of all those tiny places down there somehow.*"

I laughed. "Yep, she certainly did find us." I leaned over to look out her window with her, "I am glad she found us; you are my new world. *Il mio bellissimo angelo alato*."

She smiled at me. "*I love you trying to speak in my language; you need to learn more.*"

"Yes, I really do!"

"*Good; I will make it my mission to teach you how to speak our language.*"

"That would be awesome, thank you."

"*I will even teach you a few other things, too,*" she snickered.

"I think you already have taught me a few."

We chatted for several hours until it was late. I then showed her how to turn her seat into a bed, tucked her in with a blanket, and kissed her goodnight. "Sweetest of dreams, *il mio bellissimo angelo alato*."

She gave me a loving gaze, "*Sweet dreams to you, my silly cowboy.*" She kissed me, and then I turned out the light.

The attendant woke me up. "Sir, we will be landing in about an hour and a half. Would you and your wife like some breakfast?"

I sat there and thought that sounded so nice. "Yes…my wife and I would love breakfast; let me get her up."

"*I am awake already, husband,*" she smiled as she sat up. "*Can my husband help me return this contraption to being a seat, perhaps?*"

"Of course."

I pressed all the right buttons and got her seat situated while she ran to the bath to clean herself up, as she put it.

When she returned, "*Thank you, my husband, for doing my chair.*"

She could not help herself; she smiled and laughed every time she said husband.

After she sat down, she looked over. "*Who would have thought a few weeks ago that I would be your wife and you, my husband? I know it is not official with the church, but to me, we are already husband and wife. The attendant said it, and it was like she was right.*"

"I am a husband and have you, Alessandra, as my sweet wife."

"*And you, Nathaniel, as my silly fool.*"

We kissed to seal our vows somewhere over East Texas. Who knows for sure? She would later tell our friends we were married by the angels of fate in the heavens above. It was a romantic and poetic way to remember that poignant and special moment.

After we landed, we grabbed a rental car. I had decided to take a longer route through the Texas hill country. It was a road I had driven many times before, but it was a pleasant one. Getting to my little estate outside the city took us several hours.

As I pulled into the winding drive leading up to the house, I reflected how, when I first came into this property, I needed a chainsaw and an off-road vehicle to get to the little cottage. So many memories flooded through my mind. I stopped the car before I reached the house at an overlook where you could see down the length of the lake below. I had not seen it for a long time, and though it felt like it was still home, it also felt like it was not. I can't explain; I knew now that I wanted to remember every moment I could over the next few days.

This was the place I had planned on having my ashes spread. It was where I had spilled my blood for many, many years. I was so glad Alessandra was with me. It would be a painful and emotional process to let this place go. It was easy to tell Scott to sell it as I was not here; I could not see the trees I had planted as saplings that had now grown full. I could now see the vista I had spent so many nights staring at as the sunset over to my west. I could see none of those things when I told Scott to sell it.

Could I do this? Could I give up this place that was so much a part of who I was? It was part of what helped me get to where I am today. It was agonizing as I looked over the lake below. Alessandra could see I was very upset, and she reached over to comfort me, but there was little she could do. I remember thinking that she must feel like I did when she lost her father—wanting so much to help but not having any way to.

We were both saddened by the moment. I sat in the car at the vista until the sun was gone; it felt like I would never see a sunset like that one again. Then, just like that, no matter how much I tried to slow it down, to make it last forever, it was gone…

Interlude
My House on the Hill

After watching, even begging the sun not to set, but watching it set regardless, it reminded me that no matter how much we cling to the present, it is the past, just a fleeting moment where the future becomes the past. It is at that moment that we must capture the essence of life. So much of my life had been spent seizing on the opportunity, even though I now realized the risks I was taking were not risks at all. I had lived my life without fear, not like I had a death wish.

I realized long ago, maybe because of that moment when I was a child, that no matter how much we want to go back, to retreat to a safer place, a safer timeline…just like this sunset, it cannot be done. We can only decide to move forward. I had spent years watching family and friends—well, I called them semi-friends—become paralyzed in their own lives, whether by the tragedy of their own making or by bad fate that had fallen upon them.

They became stuck like their entire life were stuck in a bog. I felt empathy for them, but no matter how I tried, I could never get them to break free of the chains that had trapped them there. I could never understand why they could not make a decision to change their course, to change their destiny. It infuriated me to the point I would shut people out who got stuck in this bog. I would even look down on them like they were cowards.

I would always tell them the worst decision is not making a decision. Which, though it is true, was never delivered with compassion. I was saying it, but they could not hear it. The chasm between our worlds and our perspectives was too vast. No matter how hard and loud I may have shouted the answer, they were too far from my world. It drove me to a type of celibacy where I did not have many friends. I found it easier to remain detached. I could give them jobs, advice, and pats on the back, but I would detach myself when it counted the most.

I would tell myself I would take care of the financial side of things while they figured out the rest of their issue. I now see this was a completely non-empathetic, almost disgusting way to help these people who had attached themselves to me, even though I was detached from them. I weep for my ignorance and hope they can show me the compassion I have been unable to give them…

I had watched my grandmother become trapped in a persona she had developed out of necessity, but it was not her. She had grown up in a hard time, and those times had shaped her. But somehow, she lost the spark, that quintessence that is life. She was never able, except for rare exceptions, to express emotions and never show compassion for others or herself. It was tragic to watch this titan in my mind become withered by the shell she had created. She was such a pivotal figure in my early life. She gave me a sense of purpose, a drive to fuel my dreams, and the tenacity never to back down, no matter how enormous the challenge was.

But I now realize that she could never teach me love, compassion, or empathy, not because she could not, but because she had lost that special touch that allows us to connect our souls. Looking back, I see her story not only as a victorious titan but also as a tragic loss. She gave so much to all those around her, but she could never open herself up to their affection, appreciation, and, yes, pain. That is why I call my friends semi-friends.

It is not on them this incomplete status, but more a failing on my behalf. I have never allowed myself to accept any emotional input as I never wanted it to cloud my judgment, or at least that is what I have been telling myself.

Truth be told, I would not open myself up to this input because I could not risk the pain that might come with it. I had suffered so much as a child that my inability paralyzed me. The bog that was trapping me in this stone-like state. Like a rock that had sunk to the bottom of that bog. The more time passed, the more the stone got buried in the silt after years of sitting at the bottom of the bog.

Could it be found? Could my stone of a heart be found, dug out of the muck, and somehow cracked open to once again reclaim that part of myself I had buried there so long ago? It was then I realized I had never taken that risk, the most significant risk of all, the risk of feeling pain.

Alessandra had found my stone, and she had cracked it wide open. I know now I owed all these semi-friends so much more than the meager version of myself I had given them prior. I could not stop the sunset; I needed to complete this part of my healing. I was so glad Alessandra was there with me; her strength, courage, and compassion were my guiding stars. As I make the final turn up to my house on the hill, I know what to do. I pray and hope to find my voice and compassion and let them all know how important they are to me.

Chapter 18

Pulling up to the house, I saw Scott and Elise were already there. I had not expected to see them until tomorrow, but it would be nice to see them. I had not seen them in…well, over a month by this time. As I turned the car off, I told Alessandra, "This is Scott and Elise. They are some of my closest semi-friends."

"*Why do you call them semi-friends?*"

"Well, it is complicated, but let us just say I have not been the friend they deserve. They have been there for me, but I have never been there for them. I have never been able to embrace them on an emotional level."

"*That's horrible.*"

"Yes, it is, and I feel horrible. I hope that they still have enough compassion for me to let me repair this."

"*Well, I am here for you, my silly cowboy.*"

Then she leaned over and kissed me. "Let us now go meet your friends; no more talk of semi-friends."

She was right—there was no better time than the present to begin anew.

I jumped out of the car and ran to the other side to open the door and help Alessandra. Once she exited the car, I whispered, "Wait here, my angel."

She just smiled. I bolted from the car and ran to Scott. I grabbed him and hugged him as hard as I could.

"Scott, I love you, man; I cannot tell you how much I appreciate everything you have done for me."

I then turned to Elise and did the same with her. She and I had a special connection, as we were both businesspeople and highly driven characters in this vast stage of life. "You are here…I am so glad to see you both."

They both stood there looking at me like they had seen a ghost.

"Please, come meet Alessandra."

I grabbed Elise's hand and walked towards the car where Alessandra patiently awaited.

"Alessandra, please come meet some of my dearest…friends, yes, friends. Come meet some of my dearest friends."

As she walked over, Scott leaned in, "Uh, where is my friend Nathaniel? I want to know what you did to him?"

Elise snorted, "Scottie, be polite."

She always called him Scottie when he was in trouble. Thinking back on all the times I had heard her call him Scottie was so endearing; it brought a smile to my face. Elise was the first to greet Alessandra; they were both so gracious. In some ways, Elise knew I was a broken soul, and maybe she knew it was Alessandra who had mended me or at least had gotten me on the path.

Scott introduced himself, "So you are the Italian hottie, the one that has…well, done something with Nathan."

Elise shouted, "Scottie, behave yourself! I'm sorry. Scottie has been into Nathan's wine collection."

"Wine collection?" Alessandra piped up. "Well, it seems like we could all use a glass."

Scott then responded, "Or a bottle or two."

Elise cast her dagger eyes at Scott with enough intensity to melt him into a puddle. Elise turned to me, and now Alessandra was beside me, her arm intertwined with mine. "*Nathan, I took the opportunity to pick up a few things for the house. I got some bread, cheese, grapes, salami, etc. I know you like eating by the fire pit this time of year, so I thought the two of you would like that.*"

"Elise, that was incredibly thoughtful of you…and Scottie,"—I laughed at calling him Scottie—"would you please stay a bit? We can sit by the fire and get caught up on things."

Alessandra echoed my request, "*Yes, please, I really would like to get to know you both.*"

They happily agreed, and the ladies disappeared into the house to prepare some food. Scott and I followed so I could raid another bottle of wine from my collection. Alessandra made herself right at home. Then she opened the refrigerator and stood there staring at it. "*Well, I see where the sparkling is kept and some white, but where do you keep the food?*"

Elise started laughing. "Dear, that is Nathan's refrigerator. If it is not in there, it does not exist."

Alessandra looked at me. "*Really, there must be 50 bottles in here, and that wine cooler has like 70 more.*"

Elise then replied, "Do not look in the cabinets then."

And, of course, Scott: "Oh, and don't look behind the doors."

Alessandra started opening cabinets and looking behind doors. "*My God, Nathaniel, we barely keep this much wine in the serving room; do you know how many bottles you even have?*"

Sheepishly: "I stopped counting after 250."

And Scott opened his mouth again, "Oh yeah, there are five cases over there that came while you were gone."

"Well, I guess that means there are at least 300 bottles."

"At a minimum," Scott said as he was rolling on the couch because he was laughing so hard.

I looked at Elise, "How much wine has he had?"

She pointed to the two open and dead bottles on the counter:

"You know I do not drink red, so those are all his…Scottie, get control of yourself! You're embarrassing me."

Just about then, Alessandra started laughing at Scottie. "*Oh my, he is a character! He and Lorenzo would keep each other entertained all day, and I believe they would both be drunker than a skunk.*"

She kept laughing; it was delightful to see. Elise started laughing and finally went over to the couch. "Come here," grabbing Scott and trying to get him to calm down.

I looked at them all. "We need some more wine."

Knowing Elise's weakness was bubbly, I broke out three of my best bottles. Two were authentic French champagne; the third was her favorite Napa sparkling. I figured it was the best way to keep them here longer.

Alessandra looked at me. "*Should I stop looking for wine now, or is there more stashed outside, maybe?*"

Then she started laughing, came over, and hugged me. "*Oh, you silly fool, kiss me.*"

Elise looked in horror at me. Then, the stoic face completely cracked. "Silly fool? Oh my God, you have a nickname; we must let everyone know!"

She just laughed like I had not seen her laugh in many years. Before I could say no, Scott had his phone out and made a post. *Guess what? Nathan has a nickname: silly fool.* Then he pressed send and once again burst into laughter, "*Finally, after over a decade of giving all of us nicknames, you have one of your own. Thank you, Alessandra; you have no idea how many people have been trying to nickname him, and nothing sticks.*"

I was so red in the face I felt like a heat lamp had been pointed at me for an hour. Alessandra looked at me. "*Oh no, I am so sorry.*"

She lost it before she could finish her sentence and had to sit on the floor. She laughed hard. "*No, I am not, you silly fool!*"

Finally, it got to me, and I also started laughing. I have no idea how long we laughed about that, but I knew it was a good start to what would be a great evening.

Finally, we stopped laughing long enough to pick up the food tray. I grabbed two of the bottles and of course, Scott got the third. Alessandra got the glasses, and we moved outside to the fire pit. The sun was gone, but the Texas sky was clear and cool, and the stars were sparkling so bright that you felt like you could reach up and touch them. We sat quietly, eating and drinking, absorbing each other's company. I have found that silence can sometimes say more than words; it feels to me there is contentment, a mood of calm and inner peace.

Alessandra was the first to break the silence, "*Hey, my silly fool... There is our starry map.*"

She pointed to a string of stars that had formed a Y-shaped picture in the sky almost directly above us. In Texas, the sky is vast, so that you can get lost in the ocean of stars. But I could see what she was pointing at after a few minutes. If you had drawn the line from the Y down to the ground, it would have come straight down into the fire pit where we were sitting. The stem of the Y even looked like the two lines were intertwined. She was correct; it was perfect.

Scott, of course, had to open his mouth. His timing was sometimes less than perfect, but it was one of his most endearing qualities. I had grown very fond of Scott over the many years; in many ways, he was as much a brother to me as my brother. We shared so many experiences, trials, and tribulations. We were like two pieces of metal bonded in the forge of life.

"Hey Nathan," he said, gesturing like he was trying to make himself puke. It was so childish, but so, so Scott.

Elise looked at Alessandra. "What did you mean by a starry map?"

She looked at me. "*Go ahead. You can tell it better than I can, mostly because you have told it so many times before,*" she said, then laughed.

"Thanks, my angel. Well, Elise, it is a long story. Are you sure you want to hear it?"

"*We got three bottles; we need something to pass the time.*"

"Fair point, so I guess it is Silly Fool Story Time."

Alessandra stopped me. "*No, it is Silly Cowboy Story Time.*"

Scott immediately piped in, "Silly Cowboy? Oh, I got to hear this."

Both Elise and Scott had heard me tell tales for many years, so this was nothing new. But my stories before had been about grand travel adventures, places I had gone, things I had seen, and even things that I had endured. This was going to be a much different tale. As I told our story, we continued to drink the wine. They would occasionally ask to pause as Scott needed to go relieve himself.

I ended up breaking out two more bottles and getting blankets out for all of us as the air had a chill. Finally, somewhere around 4 a.m., I finished our story. And yes, I got in the Yee-Haw moment, which, after so many glasses, had us all laughing and gasping for air for quite some time.

It was a magical evening. We drank too much, so we decided to stay up and catch the sunrise, which was less than two hours away.

Chapter 19

We sat together and watched the sunrise; it had been a long time. Alessandra broke the morning silence, "*The sunrise and sunsets are different here. It seems like the sky is so much bigger than back at home. Why is that? Is everything bigger in Texas, like I have heard?*"

Then she snickered; she was still feeling the effects of the alcohol and looked at me, "*YeeHaw!*"

We all started laughing; it was so well played; you could not deny it. We all got up and cleaned up the patio. Once everything was cleaned up, Elise and Scott packed up and hit the road. Just before he left, Scott reminded me we had our closing on the property at 1 p.m. tomorrow.

"Yes, Scott, I remember," but I dreaded it.

I pushed the thought out of my mind and asked Alessandra if she wanted to go to one of my favorite cafés for breakfast.

"*Yes, I am starved, but afterward, I think I need to take a ride in the saddle with my cowboy.*"

She was so adorable when she was being frisky. We kissed and then hopped in the car and headed out. As we pulled out of the drive, she was amazed at the grandeur of the lake below. It was very still, and a fog layer was lifting.

"*It looks like you could just see the entire sky by looking at the lake.*"

"Yes, this time of year, it looks like a blue-tinted mirror, and I am constantly in awe of its beauty. Wait until you see a sunset on it, one we call a fire sunset."

"*Fire sunset, what is that?*"

"Well, they are not common, but also not rare. When the clouds come a certain way, it looks like the whole sky is on fire."

I stopped the car at the overlook and got my phone out to find a picture for her to look at.

"*Oh my, I have never seen anything like that, ever!*"

"Yes, it is spiritually inspiring."

"*Do you have other pictures?*"

"Sure, I will show you at breakfast."

"*Oh, I can't wait.*"

I drove out the driveway and the twisty road. Thankfully, Scott had not sold the Aston Martin yet, so we had to take it for what might be its final drive. Much like the Ferrari, I had been enthralled with Aston Martins since I saw the early James Bond movies. They were fun to drive and made me feel like a real gentleman.

Alessandra was nervous about my driving; she grabbed anything she could as I carved the corners. "*Nathaniel, do you know what you are doing? I am a bit freaked out.*"

"Yes, my Alessandra, I used to drive racecars and know this road well. But I will slow down for you."

"*Thank you. I did not know you raced cars. Does Lorenzo know?*"

"No, it did not come up."

"*You know, he wanted to be a racecar driver.*"

"Yes, he told me about his passion and the accident."

As I pulled into the place, Alessandra gave me a quirky look. "*Seriously, this is your favorite place. You must be joking! This is more like a fast-food place than a café.*"

"Yep, this is my favorite dive. The baristas here know me and treat me like our Rose back home."

"*Okay, but you can never tell Rose or anyone. This is embarrassing,*" as she laughed.

When we walked in the door, Valerie and Ellie were working. Ellie was the first to run over and hug me. Alessandra, being the jealous type, looked at me with that gaze.

"Ellie, let me introduce my Alessandra."

Ellie screamed, "Did you find the woman of your dreams, the one you longed for?"

"Yes…I did," I said as I looked at Alessandra, tears streaming down my face. It had been here that I had decided to take that trip, to chase the hope that there was a chance that I might somehow be able to find love again. Alessandra could see I was shaken. She pulled me to her and kissed me so gently. She had such a way of consoling me when the furor of emotions fell upon me.

I had spent so many years suppressing my emotions that when they came through, it was like a stream of water breaking through a mighty granite wall. My wall had cracks and fissures, but as I soon realized that it was still haunting me, and I was, in many ways, still trapped behind that wall I had imprisoned myself within.

We found our way to a table with a couple of chairs. The place was busy, not so busy as to feel like a train station, but people came and went.

"*Nathaniel, why is everyone in such a rush?*"

She was right. Things move faster here. I had never thought about it, but through her eyes, I could see that what was normal for me, even casual, was a chaotic storm to her.

"People here all have places to go, I guess."

"*Where are they going?*"

"Well, some are going to work, others are taking kids to school, others are going to the gym."

"*I understand that, but they just seem like they are almost in a panic.*"

"Yeah, I see what you mean."

I explained to her how Americans keep their lives very busy and how we always have something to do and somewhere to be.

"*They can't be still, can they?*"

"Maybe, I think it is just where society is now. Silence and stillness are seen as being lazy and lacking purpose."

"*Even the children here seem to be hyper. I have seen dozens run in and out in the last hour. What is it they are all in such a rush about? I do not understand. Don't they realize what they are missing?*"

"Honestly, I wish I could say, but now, watching them, I see they look more like flies than the busy bees I had always seen them as."

We sat for a bit longer, but I could see that all the bustle was unsettling to Alessandra; she was stressed and anxious.

"Alessandra, let's go find somewhere quiet and peaceful."

"*Yes…please, this is chaotic. Even in Roma, people can sit, talk, and share coffee. But here, they have no time, no time for anything. This is unsettling.*"

True, it wasn't very pleasant. We quickly left; I thanked Ellie and Valerie as we left. As we got in the car, I asked if there was anywhere, she would like to go.

"*Can you just drive? I need the motion to settle my soul. Just drive, my silly fool.*"

So that was what I did. I steered the car into the hill country and headed west with no destination. A couple of hours later, we found ourselves driving through what is referred to as the wine region of Texas. It was undoubtedly not Italy, but it was nice to see the vineyards, even if they were dormant for the winter to come.

"*Can we try some wine; some wine from your Texas?*"

"Sure, but I must tell you, it is not like what we have in Italy. Do not get me wrong, it can be good, but it is not the same."

"*I understand, but grapes are grapes, and we should enjoy them.*"

I agreed and found a little restaurant in a little town. It was much calmer but still busy, but with people at least having time to sit and talk. This was much more the pace of life she was used to. Once we got inside, we ordered some food and some wine. We talked for hours and hours about nothing and everything.

"*Hey, silly cowboy, we should be getting home! I want to see this magical sunset for myself.*"

"Oh gosh, you are right. We need to go now."

Once back in the car, I knew I would have to push it to get back to the house on the hill to beat the sun to its nightly resting place. Thankfully, the traffic was light, and I got home with about thirty minutes to spare. After I got Alessandra out of the car, I told her to take a seat, and I would get us some wine. It was a cool evening as clouds had moved in, but I knew these clouds would be a fantastic canvas for the sun to paint its masterpiece. I quickly entered the house and grabbed one of my finest bottles of Sangiovese. It was a lovely vintage from Napa, and though it was not Italian, it was a good substitute. I grabbed a blanket and came back out.

I covered her in the blanket and handed her a glass of wine. In late fall, the sunsets were almost directly over the long valley we face with the lake below.

The lake was calm as wind was still, and you could see that not only would the sky be painted that night, but you would also end up with a reflection on the lake. These are rare as we almost always have wind.

"Alessandra, I can't believe this, but this may be one of the best sunsets I have seen here. The conditions are perfect."

"*I can't wait for it to start!*"

Just then, the sky lit up like a great fire behind the clouds. It was red and orange, and the clouds looked like layers of billowing smoke from the furnace fueling this inferno.

"*Oh my, this is amazing...*"

"Yes, it is, but it has just started. Make sure you look at the lake as well!"

"WOW, I have never seen anything like this."

It indeed was a stunning sunset. We sat in silence, occasionally exclaiming as the sun continued its epic painting.

I was drawn to looking at Alessandra as the sun's epic tale painted on the sky above us ended. Her face was bright, her eyes were radiant, and her smile was heavenly.

"*Is it like this often?*"

"No, it is not; this was very magical."

She could once again see I was very emotional. "*What is it, my dear? Why are you sad?*"

"Well, it is complicated. It is true; I am sad. But I am also thrilled; I don't know how to express it. I feel so content and loved being here with you, but I am also sad to know that tomorrow, this special place, where I toiled so much of my life, will be gone."

"*I think I understand. I would feel the same about the winery, I suppose.*"

"I guess, but—"

"*Hush my silly cowboy. All will be okay; you are loved.*"

"Yes, I am, and that is good enough for me."

Once again, she knew how to calm my troubled heart. Her gentle touch always seemed to know what to say or do. It was so lovely.

Chapter 20

We sat there in silence for many hours until long after the sun had set. It had been magical; I wanted to remember this moment forever. If I could only stay here, in this moment. But as I knew too well, moments are fleeting, and the more you try to hold to them, the more you realize the futility in this. I soon turned my attention back to Alessandra. My Alessandra, with the flicker of light from the fire pit. I could see the warm glow within her. She had reborn so much within me, but I was still conflicted. I felt like teeth were biting me from an icy grave.

I wanted so badly to move on to this next evolution of my life, but the past had me in its jaws. The more I fought to break free, the more the teeth dug into me. I was in a pit of despair, but there were those lips and the wine. I sat there watching her sip her wine like I had done so many nights ago, on that first night. So much had happened and changed in those many nights. I could not help but fall in love with her all over again. She was the shelter when the storms of fury raged in my heart; she gave me solace and peace. So, I sat in the solace as she sipped her wine; it calmed my soul and gave me the courage to see this through. This endless night…

As I awoke the next morning, I found Alessandra curled up in my arms. She was resting so peacefully that it was like holding an angel who could also be devilish, as I remembered our night in the cottage by the sea. She slowly looked up at me. She must have sensed that I was awake, sat up, and stretched. Her relaxed and peaceful expression encompassed her entire person. I could not help myself; I pulled her back to me.

"Alessandra, *il mio bellissimo angelo alato*, you complete me, you have mended my badly broken soul."

"*Oh, my silly fool, I love you too, and you complete me too.*" We kissed and passionately enjoyed that final morning at the Home on the Hill; at least, that is what I thought.

It was like she was an angel hovering over me; a halo of light had formed around her entire body. As I pulled her to me and began kissing her, it felt as though my heart would explode. She loved to pull on my hair when we kissed; she thought it was nice. I had long hair for a man of my age; it was unusual, and she loved grabbing it in her hand. She kept kissing my lips and then began kissing my chest. She knew she was driving me crazy.

Then she sat up and started to unbutton her silk nightshirt. Seductively, she removed the shirt while she toyed with me by covering her breasts with her hand. I pulled her over to my side and gently pinned her arms above her head as I kissed her lips, then moved to her lovely neck. She moaned as I continued my progression down her torso.

She had such beautiful breasts, and she loved when I gave them the attention they craved. She quickly slipped out of my grip, jumped off the bed, and disappeared into the bath. When she returned, she had tied her hair back into a ponytail.

She was wearing my bathrobe with the tie loosely wrapped around. It barely covered her; it was all so surreal. She slowly walked over to the bed where I was lying. She crawled up on top of me and sat on my chest. She then pinned my hands above my head like I had done to her just moments before. Once they were secure, she slid her womanly fruit down my torso. Stopping while she kissed me and then proceeded on.

She kissed my neck and bit my lips; it was divine. Then, in a simple single move, she placed her flower on my pestle and slowly lowered herself. She slowly moved her hips, rolling from front to back. As she started to moan with pleasure, her tempo increased. She then released my hand, whereupon I firmly grabbed her and held her hips in place whilst I pleasured her fruit as she lay on my chest, kissing me. It seemed that we continued to kiss and play for hours. When we finally lay exhausted and sweating from the labor of our love, she curled up next to me. I hope we can always have this much passion when we love one another.

After our passion-filled morning, we got up, got dressed, and cleaned up. I packed the car with the personal items that I wanted to keep. The urns of my huskies, the collars and paw prints, a few pictures, and a few bricks from the drive that I had laid by hand. I also gathered some seeds from wildflowers and a few other small items. As we got in the car, I just sat, almost in disbelief. I had thought for sure just a little more than a month ago that I was going to die here, hopefully, many years from now, but still, this would be my final resting place on this little blue speck in the universe. But now, everything has changed. I was so conflicted with my emotions. Alessandra reached over and grabbed my hand.

"*You know, you don't have to sell this place for me. I don't want to carry that burden. I can see how much this place means to you; it is in your blood, and your blood is in it. I will love you regardless.*"

I looked at her through my tear-soaked eyes. "I know, *il mio bellissimo angelo alato*, but I have to do this; I have to put this history in my rearview mirror. If for no other reason than to ensure I give you my heart completely without reservation."

"*I know, my silly fool, but I do not want to cause you this great pain.*"

"You are not causing me any pain, and you are helping me get through my pain, the pain of so, so many years."

"*I know that, and I know you would do anything for me, but I can feel what you feel. This place is special; this place is you. To sell it now is like selling part of you, and I can't bear the thought of that. Please tell me if we can keep this... Our house on the Hill.*"

I was frozen like a rock in a frozen stream in the dead of winter. As I looked at her face, I could see she was crying, as I was.

"Is that really what you want?"

"*It is; I can't imagine taking this from your soul; it is a space too large to fill. I can't create that hole. I don't know if it was the sunset last night, but this place is magical. We must keep it.*"

I jumped out of the car and ran around to open her door. I pulled her out and held her so tightly that I felt like we had become one. Then, in typical fashion, "*Well, we certainly could not sell it after this morning's fun,*" with that devilish smile, "*but you must promise me one thing.*"

"Yes, anything, you just tell me."

"*We must find somewhere other than that place we went yesterday for our morning cafe!*"

I laughed and agreed we would find a new place together, a place we would know as our cafe in Texas.

We went back to the house and unpacked. I called Scott to let him know. "*Well, Nathan, that is wonderful! Ironically, the buyer also wanted out of the deal. It looks like that starry map Alessandra refers to had other plans for your place.*"

"Scott, it most assuredly did. When can you and Elise come back out? I want to see you and her again; Alessandra likes you both. Also, we would very much like you both to come visit us in Italy." They had spent their honeymoon there, so I knew it was special for them, and they would jump at the chance to come back.

"*That would be great, you know we will be looking forward to it. Now, I hate to change the subject, but I need you to decide on the cars. Am I selling them, or are you keeping them, too?*"

"I am not sure; let us see what the starry map decides."

"*Sounds like a good plan. We will come out this coming weekend before you and Alessandra head back to Italy.*"

"You mean until we head home, my friend. This will always be the House on the Hill, but my home will be with Alessandra and our Home in the Vines."

"*Excellent! You know, I and Elise could not be happier for you. We really like this new, improved version. Please tell Alessandra we said hello, and we will see you soon.*"

"I will. Thank you, Scott. Well, I guess it is done!"

"What do you mean?" Alessandra asked.

"The buyers also wanted out of the contract, so nobody was upset. This is our House on the Hill, and we will make our Home in the Vines when we get home."

"*Do you think of Italy as your home?*"

"No, *il mio bellissimo angelo alato*, I think of you; where you are is where my home is. We will create a wonderful life in the vines, and we will visit our House on the Hill as often as we can. We will make it available to the family so that everyone might enjoy this magical place."

"*I love it, and your friends and family can come and use it also, you know. It will become a retreat, a magical place for everyone.*"

Over the next several days, we spent countless hours wandering around the place, talking about what we could put here or plant there—it was magical. But now it was time to go home, back to the vines where our love had first taken root.

Chapter 21

I was in a state of euphoria when we got back to our little village. So much had happened. When I left, I went back with the mindset of selling everything that was part of my past, even my most beloved House on the Hill. But fate had a different plan. I like to think it was fate that made that magical sunset happen, like a giant conductor in the sky cueing up the music to play a performance for us. Now that we were home, there was so much to do. When we got in from Roma, we went straight to see Francesca. We found her in the garden out back sitting, just staring into nothing. She had a relaxed and happy look on her face.

"*Mama, we are home,*" Alessandra ran to greet her mother. They hugged and started talking.

"*Let's speak in cowboy's language so he can understand what I am telling you,*" she laughed.

"Well, it seems he has at least learned some of our language, YeeHaw cowboy!"

"*Mama…where did you…who told you?*"

"Oh, that would be your Nonna Alexa; she told me all about the Non-Honeymoon Suite."

Alessandra blushed and tried to hide her face behind her hands; it was so adorable. Francesca just smiled and laughed, "*So cowboy, how was the trip?*"

"Let me go unpack the car, and I will tell you all about it over a glass of our wine."

"*Unpack the car… You are planning on staying here?*"

"Well, yes, Alessandra gave up her villa, and I had assumed she had spoken to you about this."

"*Oh no, you cannot stay here.*"

"Let me call the hotel, and we will figure something out tomorrow."

"*Nathaniel do not be upset. It was just not what we had planned.*"

"Planned? Is there a plan? If so, please share because I am certainly not aware of one."

"*Well, cowboy, I do not think it appropriate for you and my Alessandra to stay here. I and Lorenzo have decided you need to move into the... What did you call it, yes, the Non-Honeymoon Suite? We have already prepared it for you both. The winery is closed for the winter, and Lorenzo and I have been going out virtually every day as we start planning the reunification. Plus, I do not want to be awakened in the middle of the night with one of Alessandra's Yee-Haw moments.*"

She started laughing, as did Alessandra.

"Then I guess I am not unpacking the car. Can we maybe head to the village and get some food? I am starving."

"Yes, Mama, please come with us and let us all get something to eat!"

"*Sure, but we should also invite Lorenzo and Nonna Alexa; they will need dinner soon as well.*"

"Francesca, that is a wonderful idea. You call Nonna Alexa, and I will go find Lorenzo."

After finding Lorenzo, Alessandra and I went to the village to get a big enough table for all of us while Francesca and Lorenzo followed in her car, stopping to pick up Nonna Alexa. Of course, when we arrived at the restaurant, everyone wanted to talk to Alessandra, and they all spoke in Italian. It was frustrating, but oddly, it was also endearing. I always imagined that Alessandra was telling her girlfriends what a great lover I was, I think. She would occasionally flash that mischievous smile, then flip her hair and continue talking to her friends.

By this time, I was sitting at the table enjoying a lovely bottle of wine, our wine. Whoa, that was surreal; the wine I was drinking was from our winery. That knowledge seemed to make the wine taste all the better. Though we still had some paperwork to sign the following day, the deal was complete, and it was just a government formality of registering the wineries back to become a single, original winery.

As Francesca, Lorenzo, and Nonna Alexa arrived and sat down at the table, Alessandra excused herself from her friends and came and sat next to me. It was odd that I was at one end of the table and Lorenzo at the opposite. I am not sure if I was the head or the foot of the table, but at the time, it was irrelevant. The point of the fact was that I was at that table; I was part of their family, and they were part of mine as well.

Francesca spoke up first, "*I want to propose a toast to our family, those who are here, those who are not, and those who have departed. To the winery that now once again is whole and to the cowboy who made this all possible. YeeHaw!*"

Everyone laughed and then responded with a YeeHaw. Then the entire restaurant all cheered YeeHaw! We all raised our glasses and drank the fruits of the family.

Alessandra nudged me, "*Hey cowboy, I think you should say something.*"

"Oh yeah," I said, not knowing what I would say. As I stood up from my chair, the restaurant got quiet. It was like I was on a stage, and the entire village wanted to hear what I would say.

"Alessandra dear, would you mind standing with me and translating what I say so that everyone can hear?"

She nodded and stood to my side.

I honestly do not have the words to express what I am feeling at this moment. When I came to your village, to that winery, I would have never thought all of this would have happened. I could never have dared to dream of it. You have all been so kind to me. Francesca, you have treated me like a son. You have been stern, but you have shown me compassion, and you have given me a place at your table.

Lorenzo, you have allowed me to be not just part of your past but also part of this new future we are embarking upon. Nonna Alexa, you have been the kindest of hands, gently encouraging me to follow my heart. Lastly, my Alessandra, without you, I would still be that lonely cowboy with a heart of stone. You have shattered me into a thousand pieces and created an amazing mosaic from all the broken shards of that stone. A mosaic of love, passion, family, and, lastly, wine!

The restaurant all cheered and raised their glasses. Alessandra put her arms around my neck. "*I love you, my silly cowboy.*"

I next looked at Francesca, whose eyes were full of tears. She held up her glass and motioned it for me to take from her. I gently took the glass, not sure what to do next.

"My dear cowboy, drink from my glass as you are now my son, and I will drink from yours."

I handed her my glass; we looked at each other and then drank from each other's glasses. I remember thinking that this was a powerful moment, one I would repeat myself later in life, but that is another story. We spent the rest of the evening sharing stories, laughing, and crying. Emotions come so easily to those who have the passion, I realized. Alessandra never left my side; it was like I was a prize she had won at a carnival. People would come over, and she would introduce them to me and me to them. We kept adding tables to our table until I think everyone in the restaurant was connected to our original table of six.

Francesca had wanted six places and even poured a symbolic glass of wine for those who, as she said, were not with us. It was all very symbolic of the bond she had with their past. I told the owner of the restaurant to bring out all the bottles of our wine he had and pour them freely to anyone who wanted. Soon, word was spreading throughout the village square, and people were coming from all over to drink our wine and celebrate the reunification of the winery. It was magical.

I had no idea what time it was when Alessandra and I got back to the winery and got unpacked. We were exhausted yet exhilarated all at the same time. We only unpacked our day bags and a few other small things and went up to the Non-Honeymoon suite. When we walked in the door, we quickly recognized that it had been completely changed. All the furniture was different, and pictures of Alessandra, her father, her brothers, and her family were everywhere. There was a note addressed to both of us on the table that sat next to the doors to the balcony overlooking the vineyard.

My dearest Alessandra and Cowboy,

Your love was discovered on these hallowed grounds and was reaffirmed many nights later. Lorenzo, Alfonso, and I all want you to make this your new home. You have healed our family, you have healed our vines, and you have healed each other. Our vines will now grow together once again, and the love and passion that the two of you bring to this place will now be in every grape that grows here from now on. I know it is not much, but I know that both of you will make this your own.

With Love,
Francesca

Chapter 22

The following day, we awoke together in our new home in the vines. How prophetic it had been that Alessandra had referred to our place in Italy with this exact phrase, even though we had no idea that would be what would transpire a few days later. As I had to meet Francesca at the governmental offices in a few hours, we got up and got ourselves dressed and ready to head off to town.

While Alessandra finished getting ready, I descended the stairs to the wine barn and pulled out the Ferrari. I had decided what is the point of having such a beautiful car if you do not drive it. It would be like having Alessandra in my life and never making love to her. It seemed pointless to be put on a shelf like something to be looked at, like a trophy.

When we got to the café, Rose saw us pull up; she quickly ran out to see Alessandra. "I hear I missed a village party last night, compliments of the cowboy."

Alessandra looked at me. "Yes, it was a wonderful welcome home celebration, and my silly cowboy was a generous and gracious host. I am so sorry you were not there. Can you forgive me, I mean us?"

She hugged Alessandra. "Of course, I know you did not intentionally leave me out on purpose, but as for cowboy… Well, I reserve judgment."

With a smile and laugh, she turned and walked back into the café with Alessandra at her side. It was so peaceful. The air was cold as we were getting close to winter, but the sun was warm on my face. I must have been completely zoned out when Alessandra sat down. "*Where are you, dear?*"

"I am here with you… It all still feels like a dream. It seems just like yesterday. I was sitting here writing in my journal about the night we first met and how your lips had so enchanted me."

"*Then why don't you kiss those lips, you silly fool?*" as she leaned in and put her hand on my leg. I remember looking into her eyes. It was like I was looking at love itself in its most raw and undistilled form.

I reached out and pulled us together with her lips and mine.

"Uh-hmm. I know you are in love, but can you please not make out on my patio? You have the Non-Honeymoon suite for that," Rose snarked and smiled.

I held her lips to mine a bit longer to suspend that moment, even briefly, to absorb all I could from the moment. Once I let her go, she looked at Rose. "*Like I have not seen you do much more, shall we say, interesting things in public.*"

Rose turned as red as her name, then ushered herself back into the café after putting our cafe and pastries on the table. We both laughed for a bit at Rose's blushing.

"You must tell me what you are talking about!"

"*No, I will not betray her confidence, plus she was rather under the influence of the wine and the cute butt of the boy she was…Okay, that is all I am saying. Drink your cafe; we must go meet Mama.*"

"Oh right," but I knew I would use the boy and the cute butt someday, I thought to myself.

About an hour later, we met Francesca at the official's office. The paperwork was tedious but critical for reunifying the wineries into the original single label. It all took only 45 minutes, but I was anxious. My mind was reeling to see the other property. What wonders it must possess, like a hidden treasure yet to be discovered. As soon as we were done, I asked Francesca if she would get Lorenzo and Nonna Alexa and meet us at the winery.

"I want to see… I want to see it all!"

"*Yes, Nathaniel, I will meet you there in an hour.*"

I hugged and thanked her. I think she was surprised when I just grabbed and hugged her. "We will be there soon."

"*Alessandra, please get your cowboy under control.*"

As she laughed at me, "Come with me, cowboy."

"With pleasure, I am all yours now and forever."

Alessandra looked at me, "As I am yours, you silly, silly fool. Kiss me again."

By then, Francesca was ushering, almost pushing us out of the official's office. "Control yourselves. We are in public, and I am being seen with you two."

She was trying to be serious, but we could tell she was happy to see us so happy.

We ran to the car, laughing all the way. I told her to drive; riding with the wind in my hair and the sun on my face was fun. I had always been a control freak with my cars, never letting hardly anyone drive them. But now, I did not care; I could enjoy the ride and the companionship. Well, that and she looked sexy with those sunglasses on in this car. She loved driving it as well, so it was a win-win situation.

I could watch the exhilaration on her face as she raced up and down the gears, carving through the turns and racing over the hills. She would laugh and smile with a beam of radiance I had never seen before. Maybe I had been blinded to this kind of experience before; maybe my demand to control situations had created a polarizing effect like a pair of sunglasses that prevented me from seeing the pure joy that others around me were experiencing.

"Hmmm, I will need to think about this more," I remember saying to myself.

"*What did you say, dear?*"

"Oh, did I say something out loud?"

"*Yes, you have been mumbling while staring at me. What are you thinking? Tell me, please.*"

"Well, I have been sitting here watching you drive this machine, watching the pleasure, the fun you are having. Thinking of how much pleasure it brings me to please you."

"*Oh, you please me in other ways, too,*" she grinned at me. "*Perhaps you will please me tonight if I let you.*"

She laughed almost to mock me, but it was a loving, playful laugh. Then she downshifted the car and floored it, racing it up the hill.

"*Maybe I will do that to you tonight. Do you think you would like that?*"

"You must be kidding, you know that answer! Of course, I would more than love it."

She smiled with satisfaction and drove on, occasionally glancing at me, smiling, and then laughing as she raced over the bridge to the winery. I realized she was taking the long way. She was having a wonderful moment, and it warmed my heart.

When we got to the winery, Alessandra took off her top and ran up the outside stairs to our home.

"*Come catch me, you silly cowboy!*"

The drive had done more than make her happy. I ran up the stairs behind her, but before I could get to the door, she had closed it and stood on the other side.

"*You are slow! Now, look at what you missed out on.*"

She undressed in a very provocative manner; she loved to tease me, and she knew exactly what she was doing to me.

Then she unlocked the door. "*Come, come to me, you cowboy.*"

It was a furious moment but so very spontaneous. We frolicked in each other's grasp, pawing, kissing, and passionately grabbing. Just as we were reaching our fun's climax, she said, "*YeeHaw cowboy.*" She fell on top of me; we were exhausted but extremely satisfied.

A few minutes later, "Hey, you YeeHaws going to come down here?"

It was then I realized we had left the door open. Alessandra looked at the door about the same time I did; she turned to me. "*Oh well, I guess everyone will know by tonight. Yeah, we will be right down!*" She hollered back to Nonna Alexa, who had come out with Francesca and Lorenzo.

When we got ourselves put back together, we walked out the door; Nonna Alexa was in the garden below.

"Well done, cowboy, well done."

It was embarrassing, but to them, this was just passion at work and not some tawdry thing. It was so refreshing to be able to express passion and love and not feel judged. Nonna Alexa then hollered into the serving room, "Francesca, Lorenzo, our lovers are done. You can come out now!"

She cackled; she was laughing so hard at us. Alessandra took it all in stride, and I did my best to hide my blushing with my new hat, as Lorenzo Jr. was the proud owner of my prior hat.

Francesca approached me and smiled, "You look a bit flush. Are you sure you're up for this walk? You might not have enough energy after what we all heard."

She laughed as she went over and sat down. Lorenzo looked at me and winked. I noticed he had two bottles of wine, and there were six glasses on the table already. He spoke up, "Okay, it is now official; the winery is reunited; we must celebrate this."

He handed me the bottles and told me to open and pour them. I poured the wine into all six glasses, but this time, we all acknowledged each other and drank our wine instead of some fancy toast. Francesca then took the sixth glass and poured it on the soil. "That is for all the blood spilled here before; they also deserve a drink."

I thought, *what an amazing gesture to have made.* It was symbolic but powerful; it unified the future with the past.

"Well, Francesca, I guess we should take a tour of the other vineyard," which was west of the current winery.

"*Yes, let us do that. We can take a cart we have an eight-passenger one that should work fine.*"

We all got up and walked to the wine barn where I had been keeping the Ferrari. In the back, they had about eight electric and gas carts. She pointed to the one she wanted to take, and we all got in. She asked me to sit up front with her so she could point out things as we went. As we drove out the front gate, I asked Francesca why we were going down the road.

"*Well, Nathaniel, when the property was divided and sold off, Alfonso did not want it to look that way. You will see what I mean in a minute.*"

I quietly sat as she turned the cart and went up the road to the west. When we reached the demarcation point between the properties, Francesca stopped the cart.

"*This is where the two properties were separated.*"

Yes, I can tell; the walls to the east and the walls to the west were the same, but for a good fifteen or so meters where they had been torn down and replaced with a newer. Then there was the dividing wall between the properties. It was of the same stone and style, but you could see it was not the original.

To the west, they had done much the same, but they changed the type of masonry and added the use of bricks to make a parapet on the corner. But what struck, even hurt, me the most was the colossal spine that ran between them. Lorenzo could see I was astonished a bit.

He softly said, "*Yes, it looks crude, even ugly. After our father passed, Alfonso was distraught and had this wall built. He said he could not stand to watch the sunset every day, looking at what I had taken from the family. It was a time of great pain for Alfonso and myself. I had never intended for this to happen; I thought I would go off and race and become rich and famous, and I would repurchase it all. But, as you now know, that is not what happened.*"

Looking at him, I could see a tear rolling down his cheek.

"Lorenzo, you did not do what you did to cause any harm to anyone intentionally. Sometimes, fate has a different plan, a different path for each of us to take. Look at my path and how it has led me here. Maybe your accident and inability to fulfill your dream were part of a grander plan that fate had set in motion long ago. Together, we can mend what was broken, each of us one brick at a time."

Alessandra reached up from behind and gave me a warm embrace. "*I love you, my silly cowboy; I truly do.*"

Francesca asked me, "So, what do you think we should do?"

"Would you mind if we just sat here for a bit? I need to walk around and feel the land."

"*Mama, you should see what he has done back to our house in the hills. I have seen the pictures of what it was and see now what he has made of it. He has a gift; trust me, he will come up with something amazing. I know it.*"

Francesca turned to me, "So you are an architect?"

"No, at least not in this tidal pool," giving a wink and a nod to Nonna Alexa.

"*Oh my, I can see you and my mother have been talking," she said, laughing.*

"Please, Francesca, I just need a few quiet moments to let the land tell me what it wants me, I mean, us, to do."

"*Oh, so you speak to dirt and rocks too. You are a silly cowboy.*"

Francesca loved teasing me, and truthfully, I loved it. It made me feel like I belonged.

Chapter 23

As I paced back and forth along the walls before me, I started having a picture appear. I was unsure exactly what it was, but I knew it would be impossible to mend the walls and not have it appear as a patch. And there was that giant scar; it was horrible on both sides of the scar wall, as I would call it. Both sides had a long dirt path that just magnified the scar wall. I really could not get it out of my head; it just amplified the pain of that time so many years ago. I started realizing it symbolized the rift within the family, the rift between Alfonso and Lorenzo. Even though it was beginning to crack in places, I knew that time was the one commodity I did not have.

I ran back to the cart. "Okay, I have something, but first things first, we must tear down all of this front area, and then we must tear down that scar, the scar that divided these great properties and divided this family. We need to get this done quickly. I think it is crucial for the family, and most importantly, I think Alfonso and Lorenzo need this scar removed."

Francesca thought for a moment. "*You are right; it is hard to see the future when all you see is the past. Let us call today and get a couple of groups of men out there.*"

"We will need more, and I will rent equipment; this has to get pulled down quickly. Every moment it is here, we risk Alfonso being unable to be healed. We need to reach out to the village and ask them to help. I know it will be asking a lot, but this is the village's history as much as ours."

We all looked at each other, and then Nonna Alexa spoke up, "I have been very quiet about all of this, as this place is not directly part of my bloodline, but the cowboy is right. This place is important to all of us. We must do this, and as our dear cowboy says, it must be done now."

She smiled at me; she had such a way about herself. We all returned to the cart, and Francesca shouted, "Okay, hold on!"

She gunned the cart, spun it around, and raced it back to the wine barn. She looked like she was having fun. I could see where Alessandra had gotten her spirit, her passion for life. It was so nice to see everyone with a smile on their face.

When we got to the barn, we were excited to get started. I asked Francesca and Alessandra to come with me.

"*Where are we going?*"

"Well, I know of one place where everyone gathers regularly, and thankfully, tomorrow is Sunday."

"*Oh, you want to go talk to Father Francis then?*"

"Yes, that is exactly who I need to talk to."

"Let us get going."

We all got in our cars: Francesca with Lorenzo and Nonna Alexa. While Alessandra drove us, with me riding shotgun. I had started having a picture in my mind, and I wanted to do the best I could to sketch out what I was thinking.

"*What are you drawing?*" Alessandra asked me.

"Hard to say at the moment; it is just a blurry vision I have, and I am trying to visualize it, and this is kind of my process."

"*Well dear, do not take this wrong, but your drawing is…how do I put this? Not good.*"

I laughed. "Yeah, I know. I lost that talent long ago, but drawing it, even as bad as it is, helps my mind fill in the blanks." She smiled and kept driving; she could see I was in a zone.

When we arrived at the abbey, Francesca asked us to wait outside; she wanted to speak to the father alone first. I understood, as I had never met him except briefly during the funeral service. After several minutes, both Francesca and Father Francis walked out. Father Francis looked at me. "*So, I understand you need the church's help.*"

"Father, I need your help. You're a leader in our village, and I need your permission to speak to the village tomorrow after mass. Would you, I mean, Father, could you please grant me this?"

He stood looking at me like he was measuring my character. "*Well, it is not typical, but I can see your intentions are good, and I think God brought you here for a purpose. Maybe you must do this, so I will grant you this.*"

"Thank you, Father." I shook his hand and hugged him, which I think he was not used to.

"*You're welcome, my son. I will see you tomorrow.*"

He then turned and walked back into the abbey with Francesca. Nonna Alexa looked at me funny, "*Do you have any idea of what you are going to say to the village?*"

"No, I do not."

"*Then you better figure it out. I do not think I have ever seen the father in this abbey allow anyone else to speak. You seem to have the angels in your corner; I hope you know what you are doing, cowboy.*"

She laughed, but she was right. What was I going to say? I mean, I had spoken many times to groups of people. But that was always about business; this was something completely different.

Soon, Francesca walked out the door and over to the cars where we were standing. "*I think we should go get some food.*"

Before she could finish, Lorenzo blurted out, "And some wine!"

"*Yes, Lorenzo, and some wine; we have much to discuss and plan. Agreed, let us go.*"

We could have walked, but with Nonna Alexa and Lorenzo, it was best to drive.

"Francesca, I think Alessandra and I will walk; I need a few moments to collect my ideas, if that is okay."

"*Of course, we will get a table and wait for you, but do not be too long; Lorenzo might finish the wine before you arrive.*"

She and Nonna Alexa both laughed. When they stood side by side, they looked like sisters. I mean, you could see the age difference, but their mannerisms and features were so similar. All three of them, including my Alessandra, had those eyes as well. It was clear they were family.

As Francesca pulled away, Alessandra put her arm through mine, and we began to walk. "*You know, she loves you. I can see it in how she speaks to you and about you. You make us all so happy,*" she pulled herself closer.

"You all do the same for me, but most of all, you make me very happy."

We kept walking; I was very quiet, but not in my head. It was swirling like a tornado of ideas spinning out of control. I could see bits and pieces, but I needed to calm the winds so they could all fall to the ground, where I could then assemble them. Alessandra was so patient and understanding of me; she could see I was moving slowly in my physical state, but my mental state was in hyperdrive. We reached the corner just before the restaurant in what seemed like just a minute or two at most.

Alessandra leaned in and kissed me. "*Are you with me, cowboy?*"

It was like I had been awakened from a dream. "Yes, I am here. Sorry, I was thinking."

"*You were doing more than thinking; you were dreaming. I could see it in your eyes, in your gestures. You are onto something, and I can feel your passion.*"

"Yeah, I guess I kind of do, but it is hard to explain, and I do not want to overreach, so I will present it in phases."

"*That sounds perfect; let us get inside before Lorenzo drinks all the wine!*"

When we walked in, I could see there were two bottles on the table. The three of them were talking, and all of them had their glasses. There was the sixth glass full but sitting alone. Francesca was symbolic; it was ever so charming. We sat down, and Francesca poured us some wine and handed me a piece of bread. "*Took you long enough!*"

Lorenzo snickered as he spoke, "Yes, it took you two a bit longer than we expected; I assume you had one of those Yee-Haw moments on the way here."

Alessandra turned red. "*Please... We did not have time for that; besides, this cowboy is no quick draw!*"

The table erupted in laughter as I turned red like the wine. I think half the restaurant must have heard her say it as they were laughing either with us or at us; I could not tell. It was all so charming, so different from the world I had grown up in; there was a sense of decorum, but once you were part of the family, even the village, that familiarity brought a new sense of belonging. These people in this village acted more like family than just neighbors. After we ordered some food, Alessandra asked me to try to explain to them what I was thinking.

I sat there in silence for a moment. I wanted to clear my head, to calm the winds of the tornado spinning in my head.

"This is hard to explain, but I will try. Today, both properties have an entrance, and I want to change that. We need to have a unified entrance, and that entrance needs to be where the walls meet. We have to leave the past in the past and chart a new course. I want to remove the wall in both directions, many meters in length, and tear down the scar wall that divides the properties.

We will put a new drive into the property at that point. It will go in and turn to the east, leading up to the original winery."

Continuing, "Then, I want to build a series of arches from east to west with a single grand arch over the drive. In each nook of the smaller arches, we will create planters to plant roses of all colors and varieties. Just as you pass through the Grand Arch, there will be a statue; I want it to be on a pedestal for all to see as they come and go from our great family winery."

Francesca was the first to speak, "*Well, certainly not what I thought. But I must say it is very symbolic of this moment in our shared histories and our shared future. What are you thinking about the statue on the pedestal, if I may ask?*"

"Well, to be honest," as a tear started flowing down my face, "it is a memory statue; I want to have a statue made of our Alessandra as I remember her that first night while she sat at the table sipping our wine. It represents the genesis of this entire adventure, and I can think of nothing more poignant. The beauty of our Alessandra and the beauty of our wine, the wine loving her, as she is loving our wine."

The room was deathly silent. I looked at Alessandra to see she was weeping, then at Francesca to see the same. Nonna Alexa put her hand on mine. "*Well done. I knew my Francisco was in you; his soul bonded with yours. It was he and your Francesca that brought you to us.*" Lorenzo smiled, "Now you are Italian, cowboy; now you are one of us."

I was unsure what he meant then, but he later told me it was the first moment he saw my genuine Italian passion. Alessandra fell into my arms. "*I could never love you more than I love you now.*"

Francesca spoke softly, "Dear Nathaniel, I think this is a wonderful plan. I will call Alessandra's brothers, and I think you and Lorenzo should call and speak to Alfonso. I think he would be happy to hear your plans."

We finished our meal and returned to the winery to discuss more. I still had to figure out what I would say in the morning. Lorenzo called his brother and told him what I wanted to do; he was pleased. He also told him I had his cowboy hat and would get it to him.

"Tell cowboy; I will make my sons come to get it from you tomorrow. If you are going to talk to the village, they need to hear what you are going to say. I am their father; they will do what I tell them to do. Let me call them all now. Lorenzo, my dear brother, thank you."

With that, he hung up. Francesca called Alessandra's brothers and told them the same. They all had to be at tomorrow's mass. Thankfully, everyone agreed; I think they all understood that the family would remember and retell this many times. The moment was not lost on me, and I felt the gravity of all the hopes and dreams that were somehow now riding on my shoulders.

Nonna Alexa and Alessandra sat with me the rest of the day, letting me ramble on about what I might or could do. They were both so patient with me.

As evening approached, Nonna Alexa asked Francesca to take her home. Francesca and I had been walking and talking while Alessandra kept Lorenzo and Nonna Alexa company. Francesca agreed, "*Yes, it is time for us all to call it a day. Tomorrow is an important day for the family, and our cowboy, our beloved cowboy, has much to think about.*"

She smiled at me, maybe a bit like a mother who was proud of her son. We walked them out to the car. Then got in our car and went back to the village to find some food. We returned to the same restaurant as the previous night, the one in the village square. The people there remembered me and were kind enough to speak to me in English or at least ask Alessandra to translate. Many people came by the table as we ate and drank our wine. I realized people drink wine here, unlike Americans who drink soft drinks. This may be why they live longer and seem happier.

We drove back to the winery that night; Alessandra just listened to me for hours, talking about what we could do this or that. She was so gracious and attentive. She could tell I was nervous about the next day. "*Nathan, do you know what you will say tomorrow?*"

"Honestly, I do not have a clue, but I always do best when I do not overthink a situation. I should speak my heart and hopefully gain their support and help make this all happen."

"*I think you are right; somehow, you always seem to find the words to say at the right moment. It is wonderful to see your mind and heart create the words and sentences as you are saying them. Even if they are not perfect, people will respect this quality of speaking from your heart. Now cowboy, come to bed, let us enjoy each other's passion.*"

She got up and walked to the bedroom, where I eagerly followed, anticipating our lover's embrace.

Chapter 24

When the morning broke, I was unusually calm; I was at peace; it was new to my senses. Ever since Alessandra had entered my world, I had found this serenity, the quiet within the quiet—a place where there was no stress, no pressure, and just being. Of course, it always helped to wake up and find her curled up in my arms; for the first time that I could remember, I was no longer an island; I was no longer that cowboy riding alone off into the setting sun. Fate had a different path for me to take; a new course had been charted for me.

Alessandra soon stirred; she said she could hear my mind working already. Once she was up, I got up and went out on the balcony. I could see the entire vineyard from this vantage; I could even see over the Scar Wall and see what had been cut off so long ago, like a long-lost child. I realized it was longing to be as much back to being part of the family as I had been. It was like the vines on the other side were screaming that they wanted to come home and be part of their long-forgotten family.

Alessandra stepped out. "*What are you thinking, my dear cowboy?*"

I told her how I felt the vines were speaking to me.

She smiled, "*Perhaps they are; perhaps fate has given them a voice that only you can hear; perhaps you were brought here to change their fate as well.*" Once we were back in the room, I knew it was time for me to get prepared. I decided to wear Alessandra's father's suit; I felt he also needed to be in the room, even if it was only symbolic. I was sure Francesca would take notice, and I also believed it was appropriate given the occasion.

When we arrived at the abbey, I saw Lorenzo Jr. and his two brothers standing with Francesca, Lorenzo, and Nonna Alexa. We went over to say good morning. After we chatted briefly, Lorenzo asked me to come with him.

"Of course, what do you need?"

"*I need to introduce you to Alfonso's sons.*"

He was very stoic and did not express any excitement about seeing them. I could tell there was some tension, which would not be easy. Alfonso Jr. was the first to speak up as the eldest son.

"*Let me make something clear: we are here because our father requested that we be here. I am unsure what your grand plan is, but my brothers and I are not interested in being involved with the winery. It has been a source of great pain for my father and, in turn, for us.*"

With that, he turned his back to me as if to tell me to go away. "Alfonso, I appreciate you coming here today, but to be fair, this has nothing to do with me, with you, or your brothers; this is about the family, all the family, and most importantly, this is about your father and his brother. And yes, I know you are here out of respect, but I hope you will respect and honor his legacy as much as you have demonstrated your disdain for what happened."

Continuing, "It is time for you and your brothers to grow up, let the past be the past, and decide whether you will honor your father and his father's before him and be a part of this chapter in OUR families and this village's history. If you are not and are simply here to make a scene, to make a pathetic appearance to save face with your father, then do me a favor and leave now. I do not believe the Alfonso I met would want your pity."

I turned and walked back, but Alfonso touched me on the shoulder after taking a few steps. I turned around. He was a bit mad, but I could see I had stirred something up within him. "*Listen, we did not come here because we pity our father; some things happened here that you do not know. You cannot begin to pretend to understand our frustrations and pain.*"

"I agree; I cannot understand those things, but I understand that your father wants this divide healed before he departs. I think we all owe that to him; would you not at least agree to that?"

"*Yes, I can agree. I know how much this had troubled him and how long it has brought him sorrow.*"

"Good, then let us give him this gift; let us come together and restore this family and the vines that bind us." I reached out my hand. "Will you help me? Will you help your family? Will you help your father rest in peace?"

"*Yes, I can see your intentions are honorable, and you are right; we owe this to our father. We will help,*" he then shook my hand.

"I appreciate this more than you know, but I would greatly appreciate you sitting up front with the rest of the family. We need the village to see this great family again, not as a divided house, but as a unified house that will restore the vines, the wine, and the spirit contained in that hallowed ground."

As the church bells rang, the village started showing up; we all went up to the front pews and took seats. Alessandra sat by me, with Francesca next to her and Lorenzo Senior next to her. Nonna Alexa sat on my other side, and then the sons of Alfonso and Lorenzo sat together on the other side of the aisle. You could tell that at some time in their past, they had played together. The tension that had hung over this family seemed to have lifted. I remember thinking about how ironic it would be in an abbey.

As Father Francis began speaking, Alessandra would whisper some of what he was saying in my ear so that I could appreciate the invocation. He spoke of family, forgiveness, and healing; I knew he had chosen the sermon with our family in mind. As the sermon was about to wrap up with the final benediction about to begin, he asked the flock, as he called them, to please keep their seats as something else needed to be discussed. He then started the benediction and closed the service. I knew it was now my moment; I hoped I would find the words…

Father Francis then spoke in English for my benefit: "*You all know the history of this village and the history of the winery. You all know the history that divided it as well. Today, the family, the whole family, has asked to speak. They are all here today, and I would like the flock to take a moment and hear what they have to say.*"

He then motioned for me to come up. I could feel my body tense up. Alessandra must have sensed it and grabbed my hand. "*We all love you, no matter what; you must know that.*" Francesca, Nonna Alexa, and Lorenzo all nodded in agreement. "*Now, just be the cowboy we know you can be.*"

I leaned down and kissed her on the cheek. We were at an abbey, so I felt discretion was appropriate. I then did the same with Francesca and Nonna Alexa. Then I extended my hand to Lorenzo; he stood up and hugged me. As I turned to approach the front, I saw Lorenzo Jr. and Alfonso Jr. standing on the other side. I walked over and extended a hand to each. They both hugged me like brothers, as did all the sons.

You could hear a pin drop; it was so quiet. I had decided, for some reason, to wear my cowboy boots under my suit, spurs and all. I have no idea why, even to this day, but on that hard stone floor with those stone walls, as I walked towards the alcove, it sounded like there were ten of me walking. You could hear my boot clack on the floor with every step, followed by the spur jingle. Without thinking about it, I was making an entrance and one that I would hear about for many years.

When I got to the front and turned to face the flock, as Father Francis called them, I first thanked Father Francis and the flock for giving me their time, then all the family members for extending me the honor and grace of speaking on behalf of the family. I then knew the time was now; I could no longer stumble over words.

As many of you do not know me, let me introduce myself. I am...

Of course, Rose would speak up now, "Yeah, we know who you are, cowboy! YeeHaw!"

I swear half the flock shouted YeeHaw right after that. I looked at Alessandra with a look of horror. Then Nonna Alexa threw the proverbial hand grenade into the room, "So cowboy, you going to tell us what you did to cause our Alessandra to become a cowgirl? YeeHaw!"

She screamed as loud as she could. To be honest, I do not know who was more embarrassed, but we both were very flush in the face. After a few more Yee-Haws, finally, things got quiet once again.

I want to thank Rose and Nonna Alexa for that great introduction. It's not exactly how I had planned to start this conversation, but we are all family in this village. As I know you're all aware, our families, Alfonso's and Lorenzo's, have reunited and are committed to restoring the great vines of our house and this village to the glory they deserve. I know I am new amongst you, but I was steered here; perhaps it was fate, perhaps it was an angel, but here I am.

You all also know that Alfonso will not be with us much longer; the ravages of his condition are marching towards the final destination we will all face. We very much want to give him a gift and give it to him before he departs our loving arms. We are going to tear down the giant wall that separates the vineyards, and we are going to build a grand entrance to symbolize the union of the brothers and their lineage. But time is our enemy, and our dear Alfonso may have only days or weeks left.

Many of you have spilled your own blood on that hallowed ground. This village is part of the vines, and those vines are part of this village. I am asking humbly for your help. Help us tear down that scar that has divided our family. I would take it down stone by stone if I could, but there is not enough time. I need you, and our family needs you.

With my final words, Lorenzo Jr. and Alfonso Jr. stood and faced the flock, saying, "Help us, please."

Lorenzo, Francesca, Nonna Alexa, and Alessandra then did the same. Father Francis then stood next to me. "I think this is the kind of healing I was preaching about; you have my support. The church will take care of feeding any that come out to help. We need to heal this family, these vines, and heal our flock," he then motioned for me to take a seat, "I think we should have another benediction; I think we all need to look inside ourselves and display the grace that our cowboy has shown here today. He came here with nothing, and yet he is giving all of us so much. If that is not the work of an angel, I daresay I do not think I would know what divine intervention looked like," he then started a final benediction.

When the benediction was over, the family gathered outside; there were lots of hugs and tears; the sons all had planned on leaving that day, but you know, they all stayed. We all agreed to meet at the winery. I asked Rose if she would please go to the restaurant and bring all the food she could carry. Alessandra said she would go with Rose to get it taken care of. I got in the Ferrari, and Lorenzo crawled in next to me; I was a bit shocked he could get in at this age.

"*Take me home, cowboy, take me home to our vines.*" The moment was not lost on me...

As we left the abbey, Lorenzo asked me to take the long drive to get back to the winery. I happily agreed and took off down the road, jamming through the gears and carving the turns. I could see the joy on this face as we drove back to the winery.

When I came around the final corner, I was shocked, stunned, even amazed; there were cars, trucks, trailers, and people—it looked like ants on an anthill. As soon as I pulled in, Lorenzo Jr. and Alfonso Jr., or as I would call them, LJ and AJ, wanted to know where I had been.

"*Where have you been? Everyone is waiting for you. Let us get this going.*" LJ asked.

"Sure, let us get everyone in the garden, and I can tell them the plan."

LJ responded, "*Great, let us round everyone up.*"

I moved into the garden while figuring out where to start. It was wonderful to see so many of the people from the village come to help; it meant the world to everyone in the family, including me.

As the people of the village gathered, I climbed up on the table where I had driven the knife into its top so many days ago. I could see the scar on the table; I ran my finger across the gash I had created. I felt bonded to that moment; I knew it had been pivotal. Just then, the table got even with me; it shoved a splinter deep into my index finger. I thought to myself, yes, *I deserved that,* laughing at the table like it was alive. I noticed that my finger was bleeding and that blood was spilling on the ground at my feet.

Francesca had walked up by this time and saw me wince when the table drew its revenge, and she saw me look down at the blood on the ground. "*Yes, your blood is now here as well, as are the generations of our families before.*"

She took a piece of cloth from the pocket of her dress, gently wrapped my hand, leaned in, and kissed me on the cheek. I was touched by her compassion. Once again, she had treated me as though I was her son. I thanked her and then proceeded to get up on the table, hoping it did not have any more revenge planned for me.

Thank you all for coming; it means so much to our family. Food will be here shortly, and yes, there will be wine, Lorenzo. There is much to be done, but today, we will start a new chapter in the storied history of these vines. And as Nonna Alexa always says, the best place to start a story is at the beginning. With that thought, I want us to focus on where we will build a new entrance, where the wall across the front was divided so long ago.

We will take that wall down for thirty meters in both directions and remove the scar wall, the wall that divided this great land. I would also like to save as much of the stone we take down to bring it back to life for a new purpose. So, with that said, we should begin, but before we do, I would very much like to get a picture of all of you to record this incredible moment. Our lunch is arriving, so let's all eat first, then picture, and then get started. YeeHaw!

The people echoed back to me with a YeeHaw; it had become emblematic of me both as a lover and a member of this great family. Rose, Alessandra, and all the family's sons set up the food in the serving hall as I got the wine out. I put wine on every table along with glasses. As soon as everything was arranged, we opened the doors to let everyone come in and eat and share a glass of wine. Father Francis took my camera and found a high perch in the rafters at the end of the great hall.

He got everyone's attention, gave a small prayer for the food and his flock, and then took the picture. Everyone was so happy; it seemed like a giant party. As soon as people started finishing up, I asked them to meet me at the wall where the two walls met. Alessandra and Francesca walked with me to the corner. I had already changed out of the suit and into my typical outdoor work clothes.

Francesca spoke while we were walking, "*I noticed you were wearing the suit I gave you, the suit of Alessandra's father and my husband today. I was very touched; it made me feel he was in the abbey with us and that maybe he was helping you find the words today.*"

"You are most welcome, and perhaps he did help me find my words; I certainly had none as I walked to the front of the abbey to speak, so they had to have come from somewhere."

Alessandra then poked me in the ribs. "*Did you have to wear the spurs, my silly cowboy?*"

They both laughed as they thought about that moment. It was a moment they often spoke about, and they were right; it was a bit ostentatious, but hey, it was authentically me, and I was okay with that.

Chapter 25

As everyone gathered at the corner of the wall, I took some marking spray paint and started marking back how far I wanted to take the wall down. A few men brought heavy equipment, which would be very helpful for taking down the wall and moving the rubble. I had decided to put the rubble in the drive of the western winery for now; there was a decent road on that property we could use to shuttle material back and forth.

Francesca handed me a stone hammer; she could barely lift it. "*You should be the one to take down the first stone.*" I took the hammer from her and climbed on top of the wall. I held the hammer up. "Let us together tear down this wall and restore the vines together." Then, with all my might and passion, I slammed the hammer into the top of the wall. I felt like Hercules as I swung the hammer; I had used stone hammers often at my House on the Hill, so I knew how to use it, and I also had learned how to choose the correct spot on the rock to make the most of its impact.

I had chosen a rock that was not on the edge but near it; it was like an inverted pyramid and was ever so slightly exposed higher than the rest of the rocks around it. As the hammer struck the stone, I drove the weight of the hammer and the power of my own body into the stone. The stone drove into the wall, and the mighty wall cracked.

The front of the wall's fascia shattered to the ground, and the rocks along the fissure tumbled to the ground below. Then, the wall buckled and started to collapse under my weight. It was a very old wall—truthfully, nobody knew how old it might be—but it was brittle, and the mortar that had bound the rocks into their places gave way from the force of the strike and the movement of the other rocks it had affected.

I jumped from the wall, not wanting to fall or get hurt. When I landed, I turned to see that I had broken a fissure that went clear through the wall and had left a gap large enough to step through. Lorenzo Sr then spoke up, "Okay, folks, it looks like we can all go. If he knocked down that much of the wall with one swing, he could surely do the rest by himself. Let's go drink some wine!"

Everyone laughed, and of course, Rose had to be the first to scream, "YeeHaw!". We all laughed for quite a while. Soon, all the men were slamming their hammers into the wall, and we formed a human chain to pass the rubble hand to hand to the waiting tractors with their buckets to take it off. For the next few hours, we continued to work. The women would help with everything they could, including water, snacks, and carrying more than their fair share of the rubble.

Before sunset that day, we had removed all the front walls and were starting to work our way down the giant scar wall. Just as the sunset was about to pass, I noticed what I swear was a ghost, or maybe an angel, hanging over the exact corner. You could see the rays of the setting sun illuminate it. It looked happy and relieved simultaneously and was gone just as quickly as it had appeared.

Everyone headed back to the village; all the local restaurant owners had left earlier to set up tables outside so everyone could eat. The entire village was in the square; we had tables everywhere. All the roads were blocked as far as you could see. We ate and drank and talked for many hours. It was magical to see the family that had been divided for so long in the loving embrace of one another. I got a great picture of all the boys that evening, with Lorenzo, Francesca, Nonna Alexa, and my Alessandra. I knew it would be essential to get to Alfonso; I thought this would bring him peace in his forever sleep.

Eventually, people started making their way to their own homes. The boys all went to the hotel, and Lorenzo and Nonna Alexa had left earlier in the evening. I sat there with Alessandra and Francesca, sipping some of our family's wine. We just sat in the quiet of the evening. Moments later, Francesca got up and hugged Alessandra and me without saying a word and then walked away. She needed time and space to remember her husband and reflect on how this day would have made him so happy.

Once she had disappeared, Alessandra leaned into me, "*You have made me, my family, and this entire village so happy, but mostly me. I could never imagine that the broken man who sat at that table that first night staring at my lips could have done all this. There are no words I can express to tell you how much I love and adore you. You will now and forever be my silly cowboy, and I will always be your Alessandra.*"

With that, she kissed me. We were both pretty emotional after the events of the day. We drove to our home in the vines, washed the dirt off our bodies, and fell into bed just holding each other. We both could feel the gravity of the moment, and neither of us knew how to express everything we were feeling other than through an embrace, a loving embrace.

Over the next several days, different people from the village would come out, and all the sons would come when they could. We would toil at breaking down and removing all the rubble from the giant scar on the land. By that Friday, we accomplished our goal. I have no idea how many tons of stone we took down and moved, but it was done. Now, the land could breathe and could start to heal. I knew we all had to return to our own lives, so everyone parted ways on Friday afternoon.

We had finished the bulk of the work by lunch, so we ate some lunch together, and then all the boys left to return to their homes. Before they left, I gave Alfonso Jr the hat I had brought with me from Texas for Alfonso, and I also gave him the pictures to take with him and share with his father.

He thanked me and embraced me. "You know, Nathan, you have given our family a gift that we can never repay. Just know that you are now our family, and you have our gratitude."

I thanked him for the kind words and assured him I had been given the gift—the gift of their love and letting me be part of their great family. He hugged me again, and then he and his brothers got in their cars and left.

Lorenzo Jr came over. "Well, I am sure glad I did not let you castrate me the day at the winery, that is for sure."

He had a delightful wit once you got past the rough and gruff persona he created. We hugged, and then he and his brothers got in their cars and left. We all agreed we needed to take the weekend off and try to relax.

Nonna Alexa was so inappropriate at times. "You kids need your rest; we have not heard any YeeHaw moments since this work started."

She laughed as she walked with Francesca to the car to head home. We all laughed; we had gotten used to the teasing, but she was right. Alessandra and

I did need some time just to be. Everything had been moving so fast since we had gotten home that we had not had much time for ourselves.

The next morning, we got up, and as Alessandra got cleaned up, I went out onto the balcony as I had done that first morning. But now the wall was gone, and though there was some rubble you could see, I could feel that the land was healing. It had rained overnight, so the air was clear and crisp, and it had washed most of the construction dust away.

You could see where we had been working, but the ground was wet and muddy, making it look fertile, like it was ready to burst forth in spring. It was reassuring; I knew we were doing what was right. There was still much to do, but the scar was gone, and the healing could begin. We spent much of the next two days just walking the properties. I had never walked all of either of the properties. They were vast, and feeling the ground under my feet was cathartic.

Even though it was cold, I often walked barefoot to feel and connect to the soil. I wanted it to be a partner in the evolution of what I referred to as our grand design. It was not that we had a grand design for what we would do, but I knew the design we would come up with would be grand.

One day, as we were walking about the grounds, I told her about the vision of the ghost I had seen that first afternoon.

"*What did it look like?*"

"Well, it was very faint, and the moment was fleeting, but it was an old man; he looked familiar, but not familiar enough that I would know who he was. I also felt warm and comforting, like a warm hug. I know that sounds crazy; I think it sounds crazy when I say it. I guess that is why I have not spoken of it until now."

"*Can you describe him, this ghostly figure? Did he like someone from your past, maybe?*"

"Honestly, no, his face was foreign to me, but his eyes, yeah, his eyes… I have seen them before."

"*Where have you seen them before?*"

"I really cannot say; I know I remember so much, but this one is hanging just in front of me, but I cannot figure it out."

"*Okay, well, when you do? Please, tell me.*"

"Certainly, I would tell you if I ever figure it out," I laughed.

We went to Francesca's for Sunday dinner; she was a great cook. The house always smelled like food, and I swore if we had moved in there instead of the winery, I would be fat like a cow. She always smiled and laughed when I said that. She seemed so at home in the kitchen with Alessandra at her side; it was like watching synchronized ballet. While they prepared the dinner, I wandered around the house; I had never really spent much time there as there were always people around and things to be done.

It was nice to be able to stroll in a relaxed manner. Francesca had collected so many memories; you could see that she loved photography, and the house was littered with them. I started looking through them; it was like looking back in time. I found a shelf with pictures of Alessandra, from recently to when she was very young. It was like running a clock in reverse; I started with the more recent ones closest to me and slowly moved my way back in time. You could tell the age of the photographs not only by the picture but also by the way the picture was taken. As I got to the oldest pictures, there was the man, the ghost I had seen on that fateful day.

I just stood there staring at the photo. Who is he? Why is he holding Alessandra? The questions flooded through my mind. Just then, Alessandra touched my shoulder, and I jumped out of my skin. I was so entranced with the photo that I did not hear them calling me to come to the table.

"*Are you okay, dear? I did not mean to startle you; you look like you have seen a ghost.*"

"What did you say?"

"*I said I did not mean to startle you.*"

"No, the other part, what was the other part you said?"

"*Oh, you look like you have seen a ghost.*"

I handed her the picture, "I think I have seen a ghost!"

"*Is this…Is this the man…I mean, is this the ghost you saw?*"

"Yes, it is. Who is he?"

"Come to the table. You should tell them about the ghost you saw; they can then tell you who this is."

I was still a bit shaken by the moment. Once we sat down, Alessandra waited until we had served the food and started eating.

"*Mama, Nathan needs to tell you about something that happened at the winery the other day.*"

Francesca looked at me with a pensive kind of stare. "What is it? What do you need to tell me?" She thought it was going to be some bad news.

"Francesca, the other day, that first Sunday after we tore the front wall down, I was standing where we had been working. Then, just as the sun was disappearing over the horizon, I saw something appear above the spot we had been working."

I described how the ghost or angel looked pleased, even smiling, and how it made me feel like I was being hugged.

"*That is wonderful, cowboy! I am sure it was an angel; they seem to follow you.*"

"No, Francesca. Let me finish, please. I did not know who the angel was until a few moments ago." Then I handed her the picture. "This is the man I saw. Can you tell me who he is?"

She took the picture, looked at it, and then looked at me. She then handed the picture to Lorenzo and told him to show it to Nonna Alexa. They all looked at the picture and then looked back at me.

"*This is the man you saw, the angel you saw. Are you sure?*"

"Yes, Francesca. I will never forget those eyes and his smile. He seemed so familiar but unknown to me."

"*Dear cowboy, you have seen these eyes and that smile, for this is Lorenzo's and Alfonso's father.*"

We all sat for a very long moment in silence. Lorenzo spoke first: "I think my father can now rest in peace. I need to go call my brother; he needs to hear this, and Nathan, I need you to tell him, just as you have told us, please."

"Of course I will."

So, he and I got up and called Alfonso in the other room. You could hear that he was not doing well, but he could still speak and listen. I told him about the angel and how it was his father, how he was smiling, and how he had hugged me.

Alfonso then said, "Dear cowboy, thank you for the hat, the winery, and this memory. I can now rest in peace, knowing my family is once again whole. Please put my brother back on the phone."

I handed the phone to Lorenzo and left the room. I waited in the hall so we could rejoin the family together. After several minutes, I could hear Lorenzo weeping in the other room; I glanced in and saw he had hung up the phone and was visibly upset. I walked over and reached out my hand to help him up.

"Lorenzo, are you okay?"

"*Yes, my boy, I am fine but have some painful news. If you do not mind, let us go back to the others.*"

He was a bit unsteady, so I helped him return to the table where everyone awaited. Francesca was the first to see us and noticed that Lorenzo was upset.

"Lorenzo, are you okay? What happened?"

Then Lorenzo spoke, "Alfonso has passed…"—everyone gasped—"but he was happy, very much at peace. After our dear cowboy told him about seeing our father, it was like he felt he could leave. He told me he loved us all and would see us again. He told me how special it was. That he wished to be buried with the hat that the cowboy had given him to honor him for healing our family and our vines."

We all just sat in silence; nothing could be said or done. Soon, the phone rang; I went and answered it. It was Alfonso Jr to tell us the news. I told him we already knew, as Lorenzo was on the phone with his father when he passed. He was happy to hear that, and it comforted him that his father was not alone when he passed. We agreed to talk the next day as we would now need to plan another burial.

When I turned around, Alessandra fell into my arms. We were all very torn, but Alessandra had been the closest to him, other than Lorenzo, and after losing her father so recently, this was just another blow that seemed to reopen, barely healed pains from her own father's passing.

We sat back down and tried to eat our meal, but none of us were hungry. Lorenzo started telling stories about him and his brother, which was nice as it let us all leave that night with warm feelings and good memories…

Interlude
In a Peaceful Death, There Is Happiness

Time is so precious but so fleeting, I remember thinking as the family gathered. Though not stopped, all the work at the property was certainly taking a backseat. The day before the wake, we all gathered in the great hall: all the children, grandchildren, wives, cousins, nieces, and nephews. There were twenty-six of them in all, not counting myself. It was somber, but everyone had a renewed interest in what we were doing with the winery. But I knew that now was not the time to discuss, so instead, they each shared some of their favorite memories of Alfonso. It was so sweet; I remember thinking, I hope someday people have this many lovely stories to tell about me. Alfonso was the poster child for a life well lived. He was brave, passionate, compassionate, and loving. What more could you want from anyone?

As the night ended, Alfonso Jr got up to speak, "*I am so thankful that we are here together celebrating my father. He was my father and a great friend to us all. If our cowboy had not appeared and our beloved Alessandra had not snared him in her web, I am afraid to say this would not have happened. My father now rests in peace, so I am at peace. Thank you to everyone for being here, and thank you, angels, above for bringing this cowboy into our family, for surely, he has been the bandage that has healed our wounds.*" We all raised a glass, toasted Alfonso, and drank our lovely wine.

As we were leaving, I asked Alfonso, as he was no longer a Jr, if he would mind bringing the family back out in a few weeks. I would like us all to be part of the future, and I have some ideas I want to share with everyone. He agreed and suggested we spend the holidays at the winery. The property we had reacquired had a manor with many bedrooms, and the family could stay there. I agreed and said we would clean it up and prepare it for a family Christmas. Alfonso asked everyone to wait one moment as the cowboy had an announcement.

"Uh, I do…sure. Alfonso and I would like to invite everyone to come to spend Christmas here in the vines. We will prepare the Manor House on the rejoined property, and there should be plenty of room for everyone. We understand if you cannot make it, but you are all welcome. Just let Alessandra and I know so we can prepare accordingly." You could have never guessed, but everyone wanted to come; I had not expected that. So, what started as a day created through death became a day of happiness, as it would be the first Christmas for the entire family in many decades.

The next day, we had the wake, and the following day, we put Alfonso to rest in the family plot in the cemetery at the abbey. It was somber as to be expected, but there was also some joy in the air, new excitement about the future, the future of the winery, the future of our family

Chapter 26

I got up early the following day, several hours before dawn. The vines are so quiet in the predawn hours, I thought. I quietly moved to the main room and sat in the chair at the table next to the doors for the balcony. I started just thinking about all that had to be done. The task was, well, honestly daunting. I thought to myself, what did I do? I know it was the right thing, but good god, man, I could not have picked the worst time to try to get all of the work done.

It was so still and pleasant that I kept thinking what an interesting path fate had set me on. I got up and walked over to the bedroom door. I wanted to make sure Alessandra was there and that this was all real and not some fantastic dream I had been having. As I looked in, she stirred and opened her eyes as she could see the light from the other room. "*Are you okay, my darling?*"

"Oh, you are awake; yes, I am fine; my mind is just scrambling at all the work that needs to get done."

"*Come back to bed, my love; come lay next to me.*" She lifted the blanket on her side of the bed, inviting me to snuggle up behind her. I accepted the invitation and soon drifted back to sleep, holding her in my arms.

With the holidays approaching rapidly, I felt an urgency to get everything in order. The workers needed to return to the vineyard to do the last-minute preparations to put the vines to sleep for the winter ahead. The days were getting much shorter, and the mornings were crisp and cold with the winter air. I knew we would soon have the first frost, and winter would be on our doorstep just a few days later. We had to hurry; the manor house had not been lived in for some time, and I had yet to even be inside it to realize how much work it would take.

But work had never scared me, so we would work. Alessandra and I would take charge of the rapid renovation; she had friends who covered most of the trade skills we would need, including plumbers, carpenters, and electricians. And then there was a pile of rubble in the parking area from the wall we had taken down just weeks before.

When I woke for the second time, I found Alessandra standing on the balcony. She was barefoot and wrapped in a small blanket from the couch. I stepped up behind her and wrapped my arms around her as she shivered from the cool air.

"Here, let me warm you up." I turned her towards me as she opened the blanket to invite my warm body to press against her bare body. We embraced and kissed until we were both blue from the cold air. She dropped the blanket and ran to the shower. I followed her as well. We warmed our bodies with the water and our hearts with the passion that flowed between us as we stood in the water.

When we finally got out of the shower, breathing heavily from the vigorous activity, we dried each other off, dressed, and started our day. I remember thinking I hoped all our days together would begin as this one had. It was romantic and exotic, maybe even slightly erotic, but it mainly was the passion that made it so memorable.

Alessandra looked at me, "*We need to go to the other Manor house and see what a mess you've gotten us into. You know that place not been lived in for two seasons.*"

"I knew it was not currently being lived in, but two full seasons…I was not aware. Oh, dear… We need to go over and see what the condition of it is."

We ran down the stairs from our home to the barn, grabbing a cart and racing to the manor house. As soon as we got close, piles of rubble were visible from the stone walls.

"*Well, cowboy, what will we do with all this stone? It can't stay here.*"

"Yeah, you are right; where will we put it? And even worse, what will we do with it all?"

"*Do not ask me; this is your grand design,*" she laughed and smirked at me. She loved teasing me, and it made me smile. We navigated through the piles of rubble to reach the portico for the manor house. As we opened the door, you could see the dust stir. The wood floors looked white from all the dust on them. There were cobwebs everywhere, and overall, there was just a musty smell about the place.

"*Let's open some windows; this place needs to breathe.*"

"Yes, that is a good idea."

We moved quickly through the house, opening windows and doors first on the main floor and then upstairs. The house had over a dozen guestrooms, one grand master bedroom, and more bathrooms than I could count. Of course, now that the windows were open, the morning breeze stirred up the dust. The whole place looked like a fog was floating through it. We both coughed and sneezed from the dust.

"We cannot work in all this dust; we need to get something to cover our faces, get the water on, get some mops and rags, and wipe this place down."

"*Yes, you are right; I am sure we can find what we need in the wine barn. Let us go and get what we need. I am going to call Mama as well; we are going to need help. Maybe Rose will come out and help, too.*"

As soon as we got back to the wine barn, Alessandra phoned her mama and Rose to come help. I packed up supplies and tools onto a cart. We grabbed all we could carry and dashed back to the manor. We had a mission, and we were committed to seeing it through. As soon as we got back, we started looking for the valve to turn on the water and the power panel to turn on the electricity. By the time we located them, Francesca had arrived with Lorenzo and Nonna Alexa at her side. I looked at Alessandra. "Well, let us hope no pipes are broken in the house. Otherwise, we will end up with a much bigger mess."

"*So, you're saying this could be a disaster?*"

"Yes, exactly. We will not know if we have a disaster until I turn this valve."

"*Well, let us see what we are dealing with.*"

I smiled and laughed back at her. "Well, here goes." I cracked open the valve to gently let the pipes fill. I had opened faucets in all the bathrooms and kitchens to flush the lines. I could soon hear the water running through the valve and the pipe attached; I gradually opened it until it was fully open. "Well, we need to go inside and see if we have any issues to deal with."

You could hear the water flowing out of the faucets, burping air and filth from the stagnant water that had been in the pipes for such a long time. Soon, the water was nice and clear, but I let it flow for another hour. I knew we would need to flush all the lines. We flushed the toilets and turned on tubs and showers. It sounded like the house was a giant waterfall, and the sounds of the water echoed throughout. Alessandra and Francesca wrapped scarves over their faces and started mopping the floors while Lorenzo and Nonna Alexa removed all the sheets covering all the furniture and stripping all the linens from the beds. While they did that, I started turning on individual circuits in each part of the house. I did them one at a time; then, I would go in the house and see if sconces, lamps, and chandeliers were operating.

After a couple of hours, I worked my way through the power panel, and everything was working beside the oven in the kitchen. Rose had shown up while I was doing that, grabbed a bucket and mop, and pitched in. The air in the manor was starting to clear out enough that I did not need the scarf over my face, but I knew once I started tearing down the drapes, that would change. I asked Alessandra to help me take down the drapes in all the rooms; it was then it started hitting me how many freaking windows and drapes were in this place.

I called it the curtain palace; they were over windows, on walls, and even used as treatments over arched passageways in the home. By the end of the day, we had gotten the rough cleaning done. The house had more than 70 drapes, 15 beds, 12 bathrooms, and 2 kitchens. I looked at Alessandra as we left the manor to return to the wine barn. "How many people lived in this place?"

"*Honestly, we hardly ever saw anybody here since I can remember. I do not think they did anything more than vacation here.*"

"Wow, all those rooms and nobody living in them; well, that would explain why all the mattresses look brand new, a few still were in plastic bags."

"*It was almost creepy, like the place had no soul.*" Alessandra remarked.

"Exactly, it was barren of any life."

Once we returned to the barn, I thanked Francesca, Lorenzo, Nonna Alexa, and Rose for all their help. Francesca responded, "*We will see you in the morning; we still have windows to wash, and we must clean and mend all those drapes.*"

"Oh, that would be so awesome; I had not expected you to come out again tomorrow!"

"*We are family; this is what we do.*"

Rose piped in, "I am not family, but I love what you are doing. I cannot be here every day as I have to open and work at the café, but if I am not working, I will also be here to help."

We all hugged one another, even though we were filthy, dirty, and sweaty. Everyone headed off home while Alessandra and I headed upstairs to clean ourselves up and get a bite of food. We were both beyond tired but felt good about what we had gotten done. Then, out of nowhere, "*We are going to be busy over there the next few weeks. There are so many rooms to play in.*"

She then laughed and ran to the shower; I soon followed. The rest of the night, we talked, ate, drank our wine, and laughed, and when we finally laid in bed, we both fell fast asleep…

Every day would bring a new adventure and a new set of challenges, but we faced them all together. We finally started getting the manor in a livable condition. We would work both inside and out during the day, and then at night, Alessandra and I would go over the room-by-room refurbishing, rearranging, and preparing it for guests to arrive in a couple of weeks. She was such a delight and so playful; even though we were always tired, we always made time for each other; she would remind me, "*We need to test all the showers and all the beds, cowboy*!" and then smiled as she continued her work and her playful tease at the same time.

It was completely delightful. She loved flirting with me, and I loved flirting with her. There was always charged air between us, and you never knew when the lightning would strike, and we would end up in the throes of passion.

With a little more than a week to spare, the place was ready for the family, but we wanted to decorate it up a bit for the holidays, so she insisted we take a few days and go to Venice to do some shopping and pick up anything else we needed. Francesca and the others continued to do some last-minute tasks, and yes, I even found a place to move all the rubble to.

A few guys came out one weekend, and with the tractors, we managed to get it all moved, though I was still not certain what I would do with it. But the place finally looked alive, and even though the vines were dormant, they seemed to also be alive. The properties were now unified into a single winery once again. There was still much to do before summer and the tourists, but that would have to wait until after the holidays. With the lights on at night and all the dead vegetation stripped from the rock walls of the manor, it was pretty beautiful. It was odd to think I had initially wanted to tear it down, but like everything else, it was now part of the grand design. The manor looked happy and eager to have life within its walls again. Like all the other things, it had become part of the family, and we were so excited for the family to see its warmth and charm.

Chapter 27

All that was left was the new kitchen appliances. They would be delivered in a day or two, and Francesca would oversee their installation. With that taken care of, Alessandra and I headed to Venice. We took her car to have room for stuff, as she put it. We decided to stay in the same hotel as before; I mean, it was where we fell in love—well, more her with me than me with her because I was already smitten several nights before.

When we arrived, she had arranged for us to get the same room, which was very sweet and exciting. Once checked in, we decided to head out and walk and live a bit. We had been working on the manor house for so many days straight that we had not taken a day off in many weeks.

It was cold, but the city was beautiful, and we had so much fun just darting in and out of shops. After a bit, we made it to a restaurant; being it was the holidays, they had a string quartet playing music. Alessandra was enchanted. "*I love this kind of music so much. Alfonso always wanted to have music during the summer season at the winery, but we never got around to it. We loved listening to music like this; I regret we could not make it happen.*"

"I never knew you liked music this much. I do as well; I love the motion within the music; it paints such great imagery."

"*Yes, it does.*" She sat just listening while we ate, and I did not interrupt. I could see she was in the moment.

After we finished our meal, we drank some more wine and stayed to listen to the quartet. When they finished, it was pretty late; we had been there for hours, but she loved the music so much.

"*Thank you for staying,*" she leaned in and kissed me lovingly. We made our way back to our hotel. We both had plenty of wine, so it took us a bit to return. We kept disappearing into dark, hidden spots for some heavy kissing and petting and then would move on.

When we got to the room, we were both aroused, but she wanted to tease me a bit more. She went in the bath and took a long hot shower, coming out like she had that first night with a robe wrapped loosely around her body and her long wet hair draped over her breasts. I smiled and playfully lunged at her as she darted to the bedroom. I quickly chased her and caught her as she crawled onto the bed. As she rolled to her back, I started kissing her lips. I was so desperate to be with her.

She pulled away from playing hard to get and rolled to the other side. We wrestled around for a few minutes before we fell into a lover's embrace. It was magical in so many ways. We had not been genuinely alone for over a month, and our passion had been pent up. Furiously and passionately, we quenched our desires; our bodies lay spent as we drifted off to sleep from exhaustion. That night would last forever for both of us in our memories, and we would talk about it often.

The next morning, we got up, both feeling a bit—shall we say—relaxed. "*Morning, my cowboy, and YeeHaw.*"

I smiled and laughed, "YeeHaw back at you, my cowgirl."

We both laughed for a bit. Once we got up, we wanted to do some shopping. I was out of clothes, and my shipment from the States had not arrived, so off we went.

"*Let us get you some more clothes, and maybe I can go by the lingerie store. Sound good to you, cowboy?*"

"Yes, absolutely, but we must also pick up some presents, at least for your mama, Nonna Alexa, Lorenzo, and Rose. They have helped us so much these past few weeks. Okay?"

"*Yes, you are so thoughtful; you know how much I love you and even lust for you a bit too.*"

She playfully laughed. She was in such a good mood; it reminded me of our time at the house on the hill. We quickly took care of my clothes and then went to the lingerie store, but she wanted me to come in this time. We spent the next hour in there. She would try something on and show it to me to gauge my reaction; then, she told me to leave. "*I want to decide how to torture you best tonight.*" She giggled. I decided it was best for me to wait outside.

"*Hey cowboy, you want to know what I have in my bag?*"

"Yeah, of course I do, but then I might have one of those embarrassing gondola moments."

"*Oh my God, I had forgotten about that. That was so funny.*" She laughed entirely at my expense for many minutes, but I did not care. I was so glad to see her happy; she could have said anything about me. Seeing her this way was such a special feeling; I could not remember feeling so content.

We spent the rest of the day picking up the thank-you gifts we needed to pick up. That night, we found another restaurant to try. I wanted to find another one with a string quartet, and after some walking around, we found another. We ordered our meal, drank our wine, and listened to the beautiful music.

"*Cowboy, this is so wonderful; maybe we can figure out some way to do this at the winery.*"

Then it hit me. "Yes, I think we can, and I think I might even know where. You remember the depression in the ground where the scar wall used to be?"

"*Sure, it is rocky, and you can't grow anything there.*"

"Exactly, but we could build something there; we could build a small outdoor theatre, we could make seats around the edge with the rocks from the wall, and we could build partial walls with arches to make it beautiful."

"*Oh, you think we can do that? Do you think it would work? That would be so marvelous! When we get home tomorrow, can we walk down there and see?*"

"Slow down, please! There were three questions in that rant!" I laughed. "First off, yes, I think we can make it work. Second, yes, we can do it. Finally, I think walking down there tomorrow afternoon is a great idea. We will make sure to get up early to be home by midday. How does that sound to you, my cowgirl?"

"*That sounds perfect, my silly cowboy.*"

She leaned over and gave me a huge hug and kiss. We finished our wine and went back to the hotel. Once we got to the room, Alessandra looked at me. "Oh darn…"

"What?" I asked her.

"*Well, since we are getting up so early in the morning, you need your rest, so you will have to wait until we are home to see what I bought today.*"

She cackled and laughed, seeing the disappointment on my face. I smiled and agreed. We packed our bags except for what we would need in the morning and went to bed. We snuggled next to one another and fell fast asleep.

We found Francesca at the winery when we got home the next day. Alessandra jumped out of the car. "*Mama, Mama, Nathaniel has a wonderful idea. Come here quick.*" I had not even exited the car yet; she was so excited. It was all she had talked about on the way home—we could do this, and we could do that—it seemed her list of ideas was limitless. She was so adorable.

By the time I got out of the car, Francesca was standing next to Alessandra. They were hugging; she could see how excited Alessandra was. Francesca reached out and grabbed her, "Okay, dear, slow down. I cannot keep up with you."

Alessandra turned to me, "*Tell her, my dear, tell her your grand design, please.*"

"Of course, but I will do you one better; let us all get in a cart, and I will take us there."

Before I could finish my sentence, Alessandra was already running to the barn to get the cart. Francesca looked at me. "*I do not know what you did, but I have not seen her this happy. Well, honestly, I cannot even remember when. Thank you. I love that she is so happy with you, cowboy.*"

She hugged me, and I acknowledged and thanked her for trusting me with her greatest treasure. Just then, Alessandra pulled up with a screech. "Come on! Come on! Let us go, please!"

Francesca looked at me, "I think you should drive, Nathaniel; I am not sure I want to ride with her driving," pointing at Alessandra, "*Fine, get in this cart now, cowboy, and take us into your dream.*"

We both got in the cart, and Alessandra slid over so I could drive.

When we arrived, the depression in the ground was a bit bigger than I had remembered. It was a good 70 meters across and close to 15 meters deep. It was very jagged, but it was certainly something we could work with.

"*Tell her! Tell her, PLEASE!*" Alessandra pleaded with me.

"Okay, dear, okay. Francesca, I want you to visualize a series of arches in a circle around this depression. Each arch would be 2 meters wide and 5 meters tall. We would roughly separate the arches between 20 and 30 meters and put a 3-meter-tall wall between each arch. Now, step through an arch,"—with my foot, I had drawn a spot on the ground where an arch would be. It would sit about 5 meters back from the edge of the depression; they both followed me and stepped through—"Now I want you to picture this area as a smooth bowl with a 10-meter circular platform at the bottom, in the center of the grand circle. From there, we will terrace out and create places to have tables and chairs, or just chairs, depending on what we are doing in this grand theatre."

"*Mama, can you see it? Can you imagine all the wonderful things we could do with this grand theatre? Tell me, can you?*"

Francesca walked around the entire perimeter, studying the ground, the sky, and the surroundings.

"*Mama, can you?*"

Francesca walked over to me. "Nathaniel, this is truly a vision; I would have never imagined we could turn this pit into anything so wondrous. Have you thought of a name for it?"

"I have not, but I am sure it will tell me what it wants to be known once we are done."

"*How long do you think this will take?*" was Francesca's next question.

"Well, between the grand entrance at the front and this theatre, I think we can get them done in 4 months, so if we get started in January, we should be done sometime in April, and the winery opens to the public in May, so we have a bit of wiggle room."

"*Where are we going to get all the stone?*"

"Well, we have it already, or at least most of it. We can use the stone we took down from the walls."

Francesca responded, "*That is a great use of that material. Well, it seems like we have a plan. We should bring the family down here Christmas Day and tell them your grand design.*"

"Yes, cowboy, we have to tell everyone," Alessandra could not contain herself. We walked around the pit for a while longer. Alessandra and her mother kept talking about all the things we could do.

Francesca turned to me and said, "*We need to do something extraordinary for the first event in this theatre. Do you have any suggestions, cowboy?*"

"I do, but I would rather wait until everyone is here to discuss it if you allow me to wait until then."

"*Of course, we can wait; it is only two days, and we can certainly respect your wish. Can't we, Alessandra?*"

She huffed but ultimately said, "Yes, we will wait, but cowboy, that means you are not going to find out what's in my bag until I know your plan for this," she laughed and smiled.

I looked at her. "That is cruel punishment for the man building your theatre."

"*It may be but keeping me in suspense is also cruel.*"

I laughed at her, "I will wait."

She looked at me, "*REALLY! You know I am going to torment you; I hope.*"

She thought I would give in and tell them. "Yes, I fully understand. I will miss out on many good YeeHaw moments, my cowgirl." Francesca chirped, "Okay, you two, I do not want to hear about this. Let us return to the barn; I am cold and getting late."

We jumped back in the cart and headed back to the barn. Once we arrived, I unpacked the car, though Alessandra unpacked her special bag. It was cute how she loved to tease me. Francesca said her goodbyes and headed back home. After unpacking, we went to the serving hall, prepared a small plate of food to share, and drank some of our lovely wine. I thought to myself; *I am so glad Sophia told me to try the wine!* That one suggestion, almost a plea, led to this beautiful set of events. Even with all the tragedy, the outcome was still a wonderful one. Alessandra continued to tease me, trying to get me to break, but I would not. We eventually returned home and spent the rest of the night just dreaming about what we could do in the theatre.

The next day was busy. The family started showing up in the afternoon, so we were busy getting everyone situated and comfortable in the manor house. They all wanted a tour of the entire place, as none had ever been there. Francesca and Nonna Alexa had put up some traditional holiday decorations to make the place feel festive.

As the day progressed, the house kept getting fuller and fuller. It was so loud it was almost deafening. Lorenzo and Nonna Alexa came over and sat with me at the dining table, mostly because I had the wine with me. Lorenzo grabbed a glass almost before he got seated.

"Do you want some wine, Lorenzo?" I laughed

"Do not keep an old man from his wine," he replied.

I laughed even harder and poured him and Nonna Alexa a glass. We all just watched everyone talk and hug. Nonna Alexa looked over at me. "*We have certainly come a long way from the first meeting when you were wandering the roads of our village.*"

She was right; so much has happened, good and tragic, but I would have never believed this is where things would be today; I could not have imagined any of this. We toasted each other and took a drink of wine. Francesca and Alessandra were preparing our evening meal with all the new shiny appliances in the kitchen. We would also all attend a midnight mass at the abbey as an entire family. I asked Francesca, "Do you think the abbey is large enough to fit all of us?" She looked at me and teared up. "Yes, it will fit our entire family. Thank you, cowboy," she grabbed me. "Thank you for the best Christmas present you could have given me and our family. We all love you dearly." She then kissed me on the cheek and hugged me. I certainly could feel her love. Alessandra was watching all of it, and I could see she was also crying. I walked over to her,

"What is it, Alessandra?"

"*You, my silly cowboy, the drunken silly fool who tried to seduce me that first night we met. You, silly fool have made all of this happen. I know we have all helped, but it would have never happened without you. I know you came here a broken man, with a broken heart and soul, but turn around and look at what you have done. That is why I am crying; I am crying because I cannot believe it is all true; I am crying because I never dreamed, I could be so happy. I am crying because I love you!*" leaning in she kissed and hugged me.

"I do not know how this all happened, but you and your family have mended my broken heart, and nothing I do will ever be able to repay that greatest of gifts. I love you!" We stood together for a few moments while we watched the entire family, being a family.

We soon all gathered for the evening meal, and after we finished and cleaned up our mess, we worked out the car arrangements and made our way to the village. We decided to all go to the village square and socialize with the people of the village, and then we went to the abbey for the midnight mass. When we got to the village, it was a warmer-than-expected night, which was nice; the restaurants had even set up tables outside with propane heaters to keep people warm. We spread out everywhere and chatted with more people than I could count. Everyone was just so genuine, friendly, and down to earth. After a few hours, we all walked to the abbey together as a village. Now, I am not a religious person, but walking with almost everyone was certainly a spiritual experience.

Father Francis could see us coming and greeted us all. He asked us to stand as there would not be enough seats for everyone, and he wanted to let the elderly and mothers with little ones have the seats. It was a relatively quick service, it seemed he had cut it short due to the number of people standing. However, when I asked him later, he said that was untrue. After the mass, we all returned to the village just as we came and found our way back to the manor and winery. We all said our goodnights and went to bed.

Alessandra and I were physically and emotionally exhausted. We could not get into bed fast enough. I told her goodnight, kissed her, pulled her close, and went out like a candle blown out by a gust of wind.

We awoke early because there was much to be done. With so many people and mouths to feed, we needed to get an early start to our first Christmas together. We raced to the manor house, where we found Francesca and Nonna Alexa in the kitchen. The house smelled amazing. Christmas here was so different from anything I had ever experienced before. It was about family, friends, and sharing, not the commercial catastrophe I considered a typical Christmas back home. It was so refreshing.

I had grown to hate the holiday, not because it depressed me, but because of all the drama, the shopping, what did you get me, and everything that went along. I did not like it. But this was different. Maybe it was because I was different. Perhaps I was the one who had changed. If I had, I knew it had everything to do with my Alessandra and her family.

As the house started coming to life, people started wandering around the manor, in and out of the kitchen and dining room. Normally, they just wanted a cup of coffee, but some would stop and talk for a few minutes before disappearing back to their rooms. It was a slow, gentle start to the morning.

Lorenzo Jr came down. "Morning!" We all responded in kind.

"Lorenzo, my son, would you go get your grandfather? I did not want to wake him so early this morning." Francesca smiled as she asked.

"*Sure, Nathaniel, you want to ride with me?*"

"Sure, I would say let us take the Ferrari, but we would have just to come back to get your car," I said with a laugh.

"*Oh yeah, I want to get a ride in that; what do you call it, Dragon? Yes, I want to get a ride in that dragon while we are here.*"

"Great, it is a plan; let us ensure it happens."

A few minutes later, I met Lorenzo Jr. out front. We hopped in his car. I often teased him about driving a four-door family car during the holiday. It was the first time the two of us had been alone.

"LJ, what do you think about what we are doing at the property? I know it is a big change, but I want to ensure you and the entire family are comfortable and hopefully pleased with everything."

"*Listen, Nathan, before you, I think we were ready to let the winery, our winery, simply fade into our history, something that we used to do. You have brought back to all our lives something that we had forgotten about, something we had lost touch with. We all had gotten so busy living our lives that we had forgotten how to live. Do you understand what I am saying?*"

"Yes, yes, I think I do. It is easy to get lost in the menagerie of the lives we build for ourselves; we get so busy just going through the motions of life. Somewhere along the way, we forget who we are; it is like we take a piece of our soul and our heart and put it in a box, put it on a shelf, and look at it as a trophy. We look at it and think, yep, I did that, or I was there, but we forget what it was and why we did it!"

"*Exactly, the passion you and Alessandra have brought back to our vines has reminded all of us of the passion we must have for each other. It is not the things we possess that define us; it is the lives we share and have touched that define who we are. You, my cowboy, have reminded us all that it is more important to love and give than to collect trophies, as you would say.*"

"Well, LJ, you and your family have much done the same for me, so I guess we are in this grand adventure together now."

"*Yes, yes, we are.*"

We chatted more as we drove down the road, but it was just idle chitchat. Once we got Lorenzo, we returned to the winery to rejoin the family. When we returned to the manor, almost everyone was awake. It was a cheerful morning; the sun was bright, and even though the air was cold, it was still very pleasant. We all gathered in the great dining room where Francesca gave a benediction, thanking the angels for all the year had brought, even the death of her beloved Lorenzo and Alfonso, which did not dampen her spirits. We all cheered when she finished and proceeded to have a wonderful morning, even though it was now almost midday, meal.

I remember thinking how odd this is; nobody is running to the television to check on a football game or some other pointless distraction, a distraction that provides no real value to the person's soul. We sat at the table for well over an hour. Everyone was telling stories and teasing each other. It was delightful, and thankfully, I had been spared any teasing.

As things started to wrap up, Francesca stood up. "Everyone, I would like us to take our cafe and go for a walk; our cowboy has something grand that he wants to tell us, I mean, show us."

Alessandra took my hand. "*Yes, my silly cowboy, you must tell them your wondrous vision.*"

"Okay, when everyone is ready, we can walk over. It will take about 10 minutes to get there, so prepare accordingly. We will all meet out front in 15 minutes."

With that, everyone acknowledged, and Alfonso Jr came over to me, "I cannot wait to hear what your plan is. You have such a gift, and it is something these vines have needed for a long time." He patted me on the back and disappeared. To be honest, I was a bit anxious. What if they did not like it? Alessandra would be devastated. I needed to make sure I won their hearts and minds over to this vision, this grand design.

When we all finally gathered up, we began the walk. We chatted and joked on the way over to the pit, as Francesca referred to it. Alessandra walked with me, and Francesca drove a single cart slowly behind us with Lorenzo and Nonna Alexa. She also brought some extra coffee to keep everyone warm. When we arrived, I could see everyone was confused about why we were at the pit.

"Please be patient; I must lay out a few things before I start."

They chatted as they watched me walk around the pit using a stick to carve a groove in the ground with sections missing every five meters—well, as close as I could walk to that.

"Now, if you please, see the line I have drawn on the ground; as you can see, there are seven sections of the circle where there is no line. I want you to break up into seven groups and stand at those locations."

A few minutes later, they had divided themselves up and had encircled the pit. Alessandra was with Nonna Alexa and Lorenzo; you should see how excited she was.

"Now, bear with me one moment. I need to position myself." After saying that, I crawled down to the bottom of the pit. There was a rock that was kind of near the center, and it would certainly do for this moment. Once I reached the rock, I gathered my thoughts and climbed onto it.

Ladies and Gentlemen, boys and girls, I want to welcome you to the Grand Theater. Please step into the theatre and spread out around the upper terrace. As you will see, there are walls between you so that you can stand with your back to these walls. The arches you are walking through are more than 5 meters tall. These arches and the walls between them are constructed from the rocks we have here on the property.

As you will see, I am standing on the stage below you. We will terrace the levels between the top where you are standing at 3 or 4-meter depth, providing enough room for tables and chairs until you reach the 10-meter circular stage I am standing on. From this stage, we will offer a wide variety of entertainment for our guests weekly—music, theatre, and readings—and we can also use it for special events. I would now like to ask Alessandra to please join me on the stage.

With LJ's help, Alessandra managed her way to the stage, the rock I was standing on; I reached out my hand to lift her to me. Once she was standing next to me:

Now that my lovely Alessandra has joined me, I want to announce our first grand event on this stage. Francesca, Lorenzo, Nonna Alexa, and everyone, I would like your permission and blessing to make the first grand event on this hallowed stage our wedding. This is where I want my beloved Alessandra and I to exchange vows and profess our love for one another. I can think of no better place than the place we are standing in.

I then got down on one knee and looked up at Alessandra, who was tearing up and speechless.

Alessandra, will you marry me here in this spot, in our family winery, at this most sacred of places?

She pulled me up and whispered so only I could hear, "Yes, my dear cowboy, you never fail to amaze and surprise me. I could never love anyone as much as I love you here and now." She kissed me, and then we faced the family.

"Francesca, our family, can we have your blessing for this union? In this spot, what do you say?" Francesca was visibly shaken and could only nod her head; all the family men and their wives followed. Lorenzo just smiled and gave a tip of his hat. Then I looked at Nonna Alexa; I could see she was beaming. She was glowing, and then, out of nowhere, she screamed as loud as her frail body would let her: "YeeHaw! We got us a wedding to plan!"

With that, everyone started shouting YeeHaw. I do not think there was a dry eye—well, except for the young children, who were all too young to appreciate it. I held Alessandra to me. "This is why I did not want to tell you the other day. I wanted this to be a day we and the family would be part of." She kissed me, and we embraced, just absorbing the moment. It was one of my most cherished memories.

As we started to leave, Francesca said, "*We must name this grand theatre, and I have an idea what it should be.*"

"Great! I have been completely blank on what to call it. Please share!"

"*My dear cowboy, this was never one for you to name, as I want to name it after you. This is our way of expressing our love and gratitude for what you have done and will do for our family and my Alessandra. I want to name it...*"—she paused—"*Il Grand Rodeo da Cowboy.*"

The place was silent, then Alfonso Jr spoke up, "I cannot think of a more fitting name for such a grand place, so if nobody objects, this pit in the ground that will soon become this menagerie of dreams and will be known as such, *Il Grand Rodeo da Cowboy.*" Everyone cheered as I sat down on the rock and broke into tears. Alessandra consoled me, "*Why are you upset, my silly fool?*"

"I have never been so touched with such a powerful gesture."

"*You should say something.*"

"You are right. Help me up, please." After she helped me get up, "Francesca, dear family, I am honored, stunned, and amazed at this great gift you have bestowed upon me. I have no words to express everything I am feeling but know I am now and forever your cowboy. YeeHaw!"

Another round of YeeHaw shouts sounded off at that pit, which would become *Il Grand Rodeo da Cowboy.* I just held Alessandra forever at that moment. The others started the walk back as Alessandra and I sat there in silence, caught up in the moment. After a while, we also started the walk back to the manor house, but it was different. I felt truly part of this hallowed set of vines, the earth beneath them, and the generations of blood spilled here.

Chapter 28

With the holidays now behind us, the work had to kick into high gear. We had so much to get done. We had the grand entrance with its new drive, all its arches, and the statue of my beloved Alessandra. We now also had to get Il Grand Rodeo da Cowboy built and ready for our wedding. We decided to do it the second weekend in June so that everyone could attend.

Every day was an adventure from sunrise until sunset. My adoration for Alessandra continued to grow and flourish, and yes, I finally found out what was in the bag, but as a gentleman, I would never reveal that wondrous dream of a night we had. Finally, my crate of things had arrived from Texas, and we decided to hire a caretaker to stay at our house in the hills while we continued to work and create our home in the vines. It was all like living in a dream.

Many weeks later, the grand entrance was complete; it was stunning, even more spectacular than I could have ever imagined. It was like the entire village had caught the fire of the passion I was carrying within me. They all brought their greatest talents to bear in the work they performed at the winery.

I still remember the day the statue arrived; they would not let us see it, so they hung giant curtains to block our view of the pedestal when it was being placed. Finally, just before sunset, they asked Alessandra and me to come out to see the work. When the workers unveiled their masterpiece, we were in awe of the beauty of the work; they had done a fantastic job of taking my mental image of Alessandra on that first fateful night and making it live in this beautiful piece of marble.

Alessandra was stunned at its beauty. "*This is how you saw me that night?*"

"Yes, and every moment since then, you were then and have been and will always be *Il Mio Bellissimo Angelo Alato*."

I had the artist put wings on her in the sculpture, and the bronze plaque at the bottom read:

Of Wine and Lips

As I sit watching her and her lips,
The wine starts to kiss, kiss those lovely lips,
Why the wine and not me, I must be thinking,
As I sit, sit watching her, and her lips

As she sips her wine, soaking those lips,
I have feelings of jealousy my heart can't resist
As I sit watching the wine kiss her lips
As I dream of her and kissing those lips,

Oh, why, oh, why can I not be that wine
When, oh when, can I taste her lips so divine,
Why not me? Why must I suffer like this,
Always wanting to kiss, to kiss those lovely lips

Il Mio Bellissimo Angelo Alato.
~ Mia Bella Alessandra ~

Alessandra broke into tears; she ran to me and threw her arms around me. "*I do not know what to say; I have never felt so loved, so cherished. My cowboy...*"

I kissed her and held her.

When Francesca drove in the following day, she saw the sculpture when she walked in. I could see she had been crying; all she did was walk over and throw her arms around me.

"*Thank you for seeing such beauty and grace in my Alessandra; you are truly a treasure, my dear cowboy.*"

She then turned and walked away before I could respond. Francesca just raised her hand to show she needed a moment to herself. As others saw the sculpture, they all seemed to have the same or similar reaction. It was a lovely sculpture…

Now, I had to focus on the theatre; there was so much to be done. Getting equipment to the location was difficult as we did not want to harm any vines. We built a temporary wall around the surrounding area to protect the vines from dust and debris. It took another two months, but we were ready to unveil Il Grand Rodeo da Cowboy by early May.

This time, I made sure we did it on a weekend so other family members could be there if they wanted. Not all of them came, but many did, and I was glad to see Alfonso and Lorenzo Jr. there with their families. We all gathered, and I asked the workers to remove the tarps they had put in place of the temporary walls we had put around it all.

When they dropped the tarps, I saw they had made one alteration I had not known about. In the central entrance arch, which last time I saw it a few days ago was not complete, they had extended its height to be 10 meters tall and had placed a series of cross beams across it on which they had placed a large bronze plaque:

Il Grand Rodeo da Cowboy

~ Il Nostro Amato Cowboy ~

I was moved. The whole place was so magical, and it just seemed to glow in an aura. Alessandra and Francesca both came up and put their arms around me as I stood there. After several minutes of silence, LJ told me, "You should go stand on the stage, cowboy. We need a picture of the gallery."

"Oh, yeah, sure…"

I walked to the stage and stood looking out in all directions, but mostly, I was looking at Allesandra. It was a very surreal moment. LJ shouted for me to smile, and they took a picture. They later complained, saying I needed to wear my duster, boots, and spurs to get the full effect. We did that another day, and that is the picture that hangs in the grand hall of the winery. But that day was for the family, not the visitors.

Now that the construction was over, it was time to get everything in place for the big day, the day we would get married in the theatre. Everything was such a blur for me; my job was to make sure the theatre was done, and now that was complete. I learned about the workings of a winery while Alessandra and her mother, along with Nonna Alexa, made all the arrangements.

My only job was to make sure my friends and family got their invitations and came, oh, and get a new suit made for the grand event. I had always heard weddings were stressful for everyone, but I never felt that. Everyone always seemed to be having fun, at least to me…

Finally, the day had arrived. Everyone was there: all the family, all our friends, the entire village, and I could not count all the people who came up to congratulate us. We asked everyone to gather in "*Il Grand Rodeo da Cowboy*" at noon. I was there on stage with my brother and Father Francis.

A few minutes later, the string quartet began playing, and after that, Francesca and Nonna Alexa walked in and took a seat. The rest of the family had already taken their seats earlier, so now the moment was upon us. Just as she stepped into the grand entrance arch with Lorenzo, the brightest rays of light streamed in from behind her. It was like she was suspended in the light and floating towards me down the stairs to the stage.

I could have never, in my grandest dreams, imagined such a divine creature. Everyone just watched her float to the stage, and then Lorenzo handed me her hand. He kissed her and told me, "You be a good cowboy, my lad, and love our Alessandra." I nodded in agreement as I did not think I could have spoken a word and was astonished. It had not been a year since I started this grandest of adventures, and here I was with her on this grandest of days.

Father Francis started the service, and within what felt like a flash, we were married. Both our emotions were uncontrollable. We had been through so much together—we had lived, we had cried, we had been through tragedy, and now we were bound for eternity to one another. We were as happy as any two people could be, perhaps even a bit more. Fate had brought us together, and we could have never imagined any of this, but I am here, and she is with me, and I am with her. We are one.

Interlude
A Life Well Lived

As I sit here in the garden at the table where it all started so many years ago, I am thankful for the inspiration of that autumn. Now that I am in the winter of my life, many of those around me who have meant so much have left us. Lorenzo, Nonna Alexa, and last year we lost our beloved Francesca. Before Nonna Alexa passed, she gave me a present. She had kept the original keychain and key to the Ferrari that her Francisco, and now we, owned. She said it was her most beloved keepsake. I can remember those days so well sitting here, and I am so happy that I came to this little village so long ago. We still have a house in the hills, and one of our nieces lives there with her family.

They have started growing some grapes on the property, which I had always wanted to do. They send me pictures of the amazing sunsets all the time. I have not visited for several years as the trip is too much for me now. Many of the children and grandchildren of the family have returned to live in the village. Alfonso's youngest son has become our winemaker; he even makes a special vintage using some of the grape juice from the vines from the house in the hills; he calls it the *Italian Cowboy.*

I recognize how fortunate I was to have been given such a gift of this life, the life with my precious Alessandra. As she sits beside me, sipping her wine, I can still remember that first night when my angel with wings appeared. *Il Mio Bellissimo Angelo Alato.*

"*Yes, my beloved silly cowboy, do you need something?*"

"No, my dear, I just wanted to see your wondrous lips." She sipped her wine in that special way she knew I loved.

My days are short now, and I can feel the winter closing in. I will miss the vines and the theatre, but mostly, I will miss my Alessandra. She was the heroine of my life story; she was…

The Panacea of Life

~ For my Beloved Alessandra ~
Il Mio Bellissimo Angelo Alato

I will be with you always and will be with you again. Smile and enjoy the life you have. You have been my greatest adventure; you are the love of my life, and I am forever yours in this life and beyond.

~Your Silly Cowboy~

Epilogue

My Cowboy Is Gone

My dear Silly Cowboy left us over five years ago. It was a peaceful passing, and I was, and I am still, bereft from the loss. We held a grand celebration after his burial in the family plot. We poured many glasses of wine and told tales of all the grand things he did for all of us, but mostly for me. We hold a Cowboy Story Time at Il Grand Rodeo da Cowboy every year. We all tell stories and share in the memory of my beloved. It is all great fun, though it is also painful. Every Christmas Day, I go alone out to vines near the *Il Grand Rodeo da Cowboy, sit with a bottle of wine,* and read this book.

I am lost without you, incomplete. I long for the day when you hold me in your arms once again and call me.
– Il Mio Bellissimo Angelo Alato

~ For My Silly Cowboy ~
~Your Beloved Il Mio Bellissimo Angelo Alato, Now and Forever~

Made in the USA
Columbia, SC
01 January 2025

50915578R00109